TIME OF THE CELTS

A TIME TRAVEL ROMANCE

JANE STAIN

ALSO BY JANE STAIN

Kilts at the Renaissance Faire

Tavish

Seumas

Tomas

Time of the Celts

Time of the Picts

Time of the Druids

Leif

Taran

Luag

To be notified of new releases,

sign up for her newsletter at

janestain.com

As Cherise Kelley:

Dog Aliens 1, 2 & 3: A Dog Story

My Dog Understands English!

How I Got Him to Marry Me

High School Substitute Teacher's Guide

ISBN: 9781521753682

To Mr. Levin
Thank you for telling me about the druids
and the blue-painted Picts
all those years ago.

PREFACE

I was surprised to learn from my mom that not everyone was taught in school about how the Pictish Celts of ancient Scotland were driven north by the Romans and contained first behind one wall

— which didn't hold them —

and then farther north behind

Hadrian's Wall.

It's true.

This happened in the first century AD. Much of the base of the wall is still there, as you can see in the following photographs.

PHOTOGRAPHS OF HADRIAN'S WALL

ONE

J aelle turned the page, fascinated by historian Elizabeth Wayland Barber's account of unearthing three-thousand-year-old Celtic mummies dressed in plaid.

"More coffee, hun?" said her favorite waitress at the diner across the street from work.

Jaelle put in her dragon bookmark and pushed her library book to the side with one hand while her other hand combed back her mass of curly light brown hair so she could smile up at Vivian.

"Yeah, thank you. How long were you standing there this time?"

About the same age as Jaelle's mom and just as quick to dye her grey hair red, Vivian popped her gum and winked.

"Not too long, and it's sort of funny watching you stare at that book so hard. Like your beady brown eyes are trying to tunnel into the pages and be wherever it is they're talking about. What is it you're reading, anyway?"

Jumping Jehoshaphat!

Jaelle only felt shy about one thing: people knowing what she was reading. Ever since John broke off their engagement six months ago and ran off with another woman he met during his time travel escapades, she caught herself wishing she were more exciting and reading something racy or even illegal. Maybe if she were more exciting, he wouldn't have left her.

But alas.

Aside from John, she was the only person she knew who read straight-up history for fun. She would probably never run out of reading material, because history was the biggest section in her city's library. She had been trying to put a dent in it for ten years now, since she first discovered the history section when she was thirteen, but she had only scratched the surface.

She put the book in her bag and pulled her coffee close to her, along with the sugar. And then a bit of mischief took hold of her, and she gave Vivian a big wink back.

"Oh, nothing you would be interested in."

Vivian laughed her hearty laugh that filled the room the whole time she walked over and got Jaelle's omelet and set it down in front of her.

"Need anything else, hun?"

"I don't think so, but I'll be sure and let you know."

Vivian smiled and clicked her tongue and put the check down with a friendly wink.

"Okay. See ya tomorrow."

Every day she worked, the bus got Jaelle here forty-five minutes before she started, so now that John was no longer giving her rides, she was in here for breakfast all the time. Vivian was good company, and it didn't hurt that she'd gone along with Jaelle's proposal that she be given what she called a 'frequent flyer plan' for break-fasts, seeing how she got twenty of them here every month.

She read the rest of the chapter while she ate, and then she hurried across the street to the museum, wondering for the thousandth time what she could have done differently so that John didn't leave her.

In the locker room, she thanked her lucky stars she didn't have to live in the ancient world. Her tour-guide outfit was a long dress, of course. Dresses made her feel so exposed, let alone the fact she needed to hold up the long skirt on the stairs. She had enjoyed playing dress-up at the Renaissance faire in her teens with John and his five brothers and all their girlfriends, but at twenty-three she much preferred pants. At least her uniform was a nice green that went well with her dark hair and eyes.

After she fastened her dragon brooch — the one piece of fantasy her employer allowed her to wear — Jaelle picked up her first tour group at the front entrance to the museum. It was a whole busload of older people, which made her smile. They were generally more appreciative of the historical artifacts. And more forgiving when she shot off her mouth, as she was wont to do. She knew her mouth was a problem, but she just couldn't seem to help herself. She honestly didn't notice she was saying most of the stuff her mouth came up with until it was too late. It mostly took off on a rant when she got anxious about something, so she tried to avoid those situations.

But life happens whether you want it to or not.

"Welcome to the Museum of Ancient History. I'm Jaelle Penzag, and I'll be your guide today. The museum has enough exhibits for a week of tours, so give me some ideas. Is there anything you especially want to see?"

A white-haired chubby grandpa came up.

"I especially want to see the Scottish exhibit, but Penzag is a Jewish name, isn't it? What would you know about the Celts?"

Jaelle saw red. Did the old man really think that way in this day and age?

"I happen to know quite a lot about the Celts, thank you for asking. For example, did you know that the Scots are only one of the Celtic peoples? I'm reading a really good book right now about three thousand year old Celtic burial sites that were unearthed all around the Baltic Sea. If that holds your curiosity," she glanced at everyone in the group to include them too, "until the end of this tour, then please ask me and I'll give you the details of the book. It's really good. I highly recommend it. And that's not the only book I've read about the Celts. Our city's library has 268 such books, and so far I've read 57 of them. And that's just one people group I've read about. It's amazing what you can find out if you seek out the information from reliable sources and don't just go on your own personal instincts and beliefs and prejudices. That's such a closed-minded and narrow view of the world that it won't serve you well..."

At this point, Jaelle realized she was running her mouth again and shut up. She led the group toward the Celtic section first, calling out to the janitor as she passed him by.

"Cinnead! Come with us. We need to do a demonstration for these folks."

Older himself — probably fifty or so — Cinnead got a big grin on his face and put down his mop as he followed them into the big room with all the weapons on the walls. He donned his helmet and padded jerkin — similar to the lead apron the dentist had you wear when he took x-rays, but covering front and back — and took down their two padded demonstration swords and held hers out to her by the handle. This was why both of them had kept their jobs through the recent reorganization of the museum: they were both fighting members of the Society for Creative Anachronism, and the museum patrons loved to watch them practice.

Hitching up her long skirt into her belt so that it was only knee-length, she donned her own helmet and padded jerkin — a Chinese one with dragons on it — then looked up at the tour group and gestured back behind the ropes.

"Please move to the perimeter of the room behind those ropes and then we'll give you a demonstration of some of these weapons, okay?"

The museum patrons always loved the sword demonstrations, and the older patrons more than the rest. Some of them whistled and clapped, and everyone cheered.

Except chubby grandpa. He stood over in the corner by himself, looking ticked off.

Meanwhile, in the center of the room, Cinnead came at Jaelle with his huge practice sword over his head, ready to hack down on top of her.

Jaelle raised up her own practice sword, parrying his attack and then hitting his padded stomach with her sword's handle.

They went back and forth like that a dozen times to cheers and applause from most of the tour group. But chubby grandpa just stood there in the corner with a sour face.

Jaelle held up her hand, and Cinnead stopped. Then she went over to chubby grandpa and put the sword down tip first and leaned on the handle toward him.

"You mean to tell me not even this demonstration has impressed you?"

He looked cross at her.

"Oh, you obviously rehearsed this ahead of time. You wouldn't stand a chance in a real fight, a skinny little Jewish girl like you."

Seeing red again but hanging on to her composure by a thread, Jaelle motioned Cinnead over and took his sword and padded jerkin from him, then held them out to chubby grandpa.

"Are you saying you could do better?"

Chubby got an evil look in his eyes as he shook his head and waved the sword away.

"Naw, you don't want to mess with a man in a real fight."

Jaelle crossed her arms, lifting the sword up beside her with one hand.

"Oh, it won't be a real fight. We'll just fight to touch, not harm. Right?"

Chubby got that evil look in his eyes again.

"Right."

Jaelle held the rope up for Chubby and motioned him into the center of the room. As she did so, all the side conversations quieted down and a hush came over the room. Jaelle found Cinnead's eyes and motioned with her own over to a net on the wall. Cinnead nodded his understanding and quietly went over and got it and stood ready. She was glad he was there, just in case.

A kind-faced grandma spoke up with the commanding air of a teacher.

"This is too dangerous, dear. This gentleman should just be shown out. You need to call whatever security you have here." She looked around at the men around her. "Or perhaps some of these gentlemen could help us out and escort him downstairs to the bus, where he can wait for the rest of us without causing any further trouble."

The men around her nodded, and she and they started to go under the ropes toward chubby grandpa.

Jaelle stepped in front of them and held her sword out to block their way.

"It's really no trouble at all." She turned to chubby, who had donned Cinnead's helmet and padded jerkin. "You'll need to sign this liability waiver."

He grabbed it, gave it a quick read and scribble, then held it out for her to take.

She motioned to Cinnead, who strode up with the net in his hand, perused the waiver, and nodded in affirmation that it was signed before he went back to the sidelines.

She raised her chin up at chubby grandpa.

"Ready?"

The evil glint in Chubby's eyes showed even from all the way across the room as he readied his battle stance and took his sword up in both hands and held it like a baseball bat.

Jaelle did her best not to smile on the outside as much as she was smiling on the inside. Chubby's stance was all wrong. This was going to be even easier than she thought. Taking her own battle stance, she nodded at chubby.

"Come at me whenever you're ready."

Chubby didn't waste any time. He ran at her like Cinnead had — only his form was all wrong.

Instead of parrying his attack, Jaelle lowered her sword, ducked under his sword, and mimed a slice along his midsection as she ran past him, then quickly pivoted so that she was facing him again. They ran past each other four times in this manner, and each time he didn't even get a hit in, while she mimed slicing him in both arms and his left leg. After just those four times, he was panting.

She was still calm, cool, and collected.

"My turn."

The faces of everyone around the perimeter of the

room opened up in shock at the prospect of her charging an exhausted defenseless man.

Jaelle ran in with her sword raised high, but at the last moment she sideswiped straight at chubby grandpa's sword, knocking it out of his hands so that it slid across the floor straight into Cinnead's reach. Cinnead picked it up with a flourish, which made everyone clap and laugh.

So Cinnead took a bow.

After the tourists were done clapping for him, they turned to Jaelle and clapped some more for her before they quieted down again and looked at her expectantly.

Jaelle opened the rope into the next room and smiled at everyone as they went by. Except for Chubby.

She stood in his way and gave Chubby a serious face as she spoke quietly, for his ears only.

"We're everywhere."

TWO

Breth mac Eddarrnonn pulled back the branches of the bush on either side of his pale woad-coated face and brushed back his short ash-blond hair. He wanted to see down the hill toward the Roman fort. It lay just on the other side of the long Roman wall that would soon span all the way across the land, the way construction was going, from the Norse Sea to the Gaelic Sea. Confident that the blue designs all over his naked body would camouflage him in the darkness, he laughed to himself as he watched a dozen Roman soldiers march up and down the other side of the wall in formation.

Not only were the barbarians' movements against nature and thus inadvisable on principle, but also they were foolish strategically. When they came to the end of their march and all turned around at the same time, they made it too easy for Breth to creep through the next break in the bushes down the hill without being seen even if he hadn't been camouflaged. And on to the next gap between bushes. And the next.

He had to suppress his laugh lest they hear him. The savages were asking to be raided. He was just one man this night, here only to scout, but soon he would come back with every fighter in his clan, who would all have time to creep down this hill undetected, so stupid were the invaders and their wall. It could not be allowed to be finished. Even though it was easily climbed by people, it would block the natural migrations of many animals and make game dangerously scarce.

When at last Breth reached the barbarians' wall, he easily climbed the ten feet to the top using the wall's own stones as hand and footholds. Hidden up there by the branches of a nearby tree, he scouted out the fort to his satisfaction, reckoning how many soldiers were inside, where they slept, and where the fat leader sat talking and eating with his team leaders.

These savages were so confident in the power of this flat square fortress they had made that they even had music at supper time. They felt safe and secure enough to broadcast their location to everyone for miles around through the music of their bagpipes.

Oh, to be sure, Breth's people had bagpipes too. As did the Angles and the Saxons. Everybody did — except the Gaels. But the Picts seldom were able to play their pipes, relying on stealth warfare as they did.

These so-called Romans, however, flaunted their bagpipes. They played their strange tunes long and often, as if to declare to the rest of the island 'We Romans are here to stay! You shall not be rid of us!' These cocky invaders even piped their signals in battle, undaunted by the prospect of their enemies also hearing their signals. Sheer arrogance.

Comfortable in his perch on top of the wall under the tree – and completely without the need for food or rest — Breth sipped from his water skin all night, waiting to see how close to sunrise it was when these dozen guards went in and a dozen fresh guards came out.

Once he had observed all he felt he needed to, Breth took from a small bag attached to his water skin the hammer and chisel his brother Talorc had made at the forge in their far-off village home and got to work drawing symbols into the top row of stones in the wall.

He didn't always chisel exactly the same sequence of pictures, but it was a version of the same story any other self-respecting Pictish Celt would have carved in the savages' wall, given the opportunity. His pictures told how the invaders had come and driven the Picts and the other Celts of these islands so far north that there was barely any arable land. They showed the stories of all the Celtic resistances, each raid on the impostors south of the wall pictured out in curly symbols. His carvings boasted how the impostors owed the Picts in particular a great debt for all the land they had claimed for themselves alone, and symbolically Breth promised that one day, the invaders would be made to repay this debt.

As did every stone carver, Breth added his own personal touch. He chiseled out in graphic detail how the impostors had taken the life of his dear Caitlin. And just as graphically, he portrayed all the ways he would avenge her.

Breth was in the middle of creating an especially beautiful flourish of bush leaves around his face at his favorite lookout point when he realized the mistake he had made in getting too involved in his storytelling.

Two arrows came whistling toward him, and more had been loosed but gone astray, judging by the sounds he heard. The next volley likely wouldn't miss.

Cursing, he jumped down from the wall with his tools in his hands and turned to run back up the hill — only to find the entire dozen guards coming around the end of the wall at the gate opening.

Casting the tools aside, Breth reached overhead and grabbed his large two-handed sword out of the sheath he wore on his back as he ran up the hill to the first break in the bushes. Once he got through, he turned and jumped on top of the first guard, who was forced to come at him alone, so narrow was the passage.

Duly surprised, the first guard fell, creating a barrier for his fellows and buying Breth time to run up the hill to his next pre-selected ambush point. And so on it went until he neared the top.

Cursing at himself again for getting carried away with his stone carving and losing track of the bigger plan — scout out the fort now and come back with all the fighters in the clan later — Breth prematurely pulled the rope that loosed the stones he and his clan had stockpiled up here. They were intended for a raid, but now he was wasting them on a personal escape after a scouting trip that had already been over.

Disappointed that he couldn't take the time to look over his shoulder and see how many barbarians he killed with his avalanche, Breth dove off the other side of the hill into a river and swam away.

THREE

At home the evening after her skirmish with chubby grandpa, Jaelle guzzled a few beers. She needed to work up the courage to go through the boxes John had left in the basement of the house they were going to share together in their married life — before he found another woman and ran off. Amid all this clutter, maybe there was something valuable that she could sell. Hopefully she wouldn't find some other woman's lingerie. Ew.

She was opening the first box when her phone buzzed. It was one of her and John's old friends.

Should she answer?

It was Amber, Jaelle's oldest woman friend she still kept in touch with. Amber had gone to Scotland in order to hopefully get back together with Tomas, who was John's uncle and another of Jaelle's old friends.

And if Amber had good news about that?

Ug. If Amber was back together with Tomas, Jaelle didn't want to suffer through hearing all about it.

She had just decided to ignore the call when out of habit, her finger hit 'answer.'

And man oh Manischewitz, Amber's story was even worse than Jaelle feared.

Amber gave her a romantic story about traveling into the past with her old boyfriend Tomas, saving the man from the enchanting spell of a druidess — and then getting married to him. They were married.

She went on.

And on.

And on.

Amber and Kelsey and some friends of theirs had a quadruple wedding. And of course John had attended. With his new woman. Who was 'gorgeous in that old-fashioned kind of way, you know, emphasizing femininity and dependence on a man.'

Gag.

Jaelle make choking sounds.

But there was no getting through to Amber. She didn't even miss a beat.

"Yeah, the Scottish skies were sunny for once, and we had a beautiful old time wedding on the cliff overlooking the Irish Sea—and then we all high-tailed it back here to the present."

How dare Amber go on and on and on about this?

She knew how brokenhearted Jaelle was over losing her precious Tomas's nephew of the same age as him, John.

Amber's inconsideration chuffed, and so Jaelle lashed out at her oldest friend. But it wasn't Jaelle's way to be direct. She didn't just tell Amber 'Quit being rude.' No. She wanted it to slowly sink in, to gradually dawn on her friend that she was being rude.

That way, the guilt would go in deeper.

And so Jaelle nit-picked Amber's wedding story, pointing out things for Amber to worry about — in the hope that she would be very worried, indeed. That it would rain on her parade. Ruin her fun. Spoil her oh-so-sunshiny mood.

"But no one in the present knew you were married, and no time had passed in order for you to get married in. How did you deal with that?"

Amber laughed.

That wasn't the reaction Jaelle hoped for, but good that Amber was finally going to quit being so darn romantic and maybe even give her friend some much-needed sympathy. Maybe this was better.

Looking forward to some actual companionship and a figurative shoulder to cry on, Jaelle spoke up hopefully.

"Must be thinking of a good story."

"No, no. I was laughing because I splattered some nail polish."

You've got to be kidding me.

"Huh?"

"It could've gotten on the pillowcase if it weren't for this paper towel, and at first I was really upset, you know? But I was laughing because it occurred to me that with the amount Mr. Blair is paying me for helping Kelsey out with her cataloging system for the archaeological dig here, I could buy a thousand pillowcases, so what am I worried about?"

Yeah, what was Amber worried about? Certainly not about bragging she had more money than Jaelle would ever see. Or that Amber had married her longtime boyfriend when Jaelle had lost hers. Or about how Amber was really fulfilled in the work that she was doing while Jaelle still worked an entry level job at the museum.

Yeah, guilting Amber was so much better an idea.

Jaelle laughed a sarcastic 'ha ha' kind of laugh, expecting Amber to say 'what?' and then realize what a terrible friend she was being.

But Amber was so full of herself right now she didn't hear the ironic part and laughed along in pleasure.

Feh. Time for some directness.

Before words came out that might be regretted later. Maybe.

Jaelle cleared her throat.

Amber snorted.

"Okay, okay, I'll get back to my story. I know you don't want to hear about nail polish—"

Wanna bet? Without the money bragging, that would be much better than your wedding story.

But Amber went on, still full of herself.

"We made our marriage legal two days after we got back to the present. We just flew back home and saw a justice of the peace."

Once more, Jaelle tried sarcasm.

"Aw, that's too bad—"

But Amber was oblivious.

"No, I wanted it that way. Over and done with as quickly as possible so we could get on with married life, already—"

Maybe it was the beer talking, but at that, Jaelle burst into a loud peal of genuine laughter.

Amber growled at her playfully.

"Oh, would you get your mind out of the gutter for once? My family were all there to witness my happiness, and getting married to Tomas was all that really mattered to me. It wasn't about the dress, or the ring, or having to dance to a certain song at a reception, cutting the cake, throwing the bouquet, riding in a limousine, or picking out bridesmaids' dresses. It was about declaring in front of witnesses our intention to spend the rest of our lives together as husband and wife."

Ugh.

Way to ruin the happy mood.

Could Amber be any more selfishly chipper? Time to rain on her parade again. She was at work and couldn't get away, right? A good dig at that might snap some sense into the selfish brat — whose company Jaelle desperately wanted, she knew deep down, or she would have just told her friend off and hung up.

"Did you at least get a honeymoon?"

To her credit, Amber paused a bit, showing that she'd heard at least a little of Jaelle's tone. But then she droned on again about how happy she was.

"Tavish & Kelsey and Seumas & Sasha had plane

tickets to Hawaii already, so they were all gone for two weeks. Me and Tomas were bummed we couldn't go along — until Mr. Blair showed up with the motorboat he'd been promising everyone."

And that did it. Jaelle burst into tears. Whenever she did that, her nose ran. She blew it on her T-shirt.

"Wow, cool."

Amber blathered on some more, obviously unaware of the pain she was causing. Because Amber wasn't mean, just recently married and deliriously happy.

Feh.

"You can say that again. The motorboat has a cabin and everything, and when he heard we just got married, he let us take it over to Ireland for a week, all by ourselves. We docked at a different port every night and went sight-seeing every day, not to mention all the pub crawling we did. Couldn't have planned a better honeymoon if I tried. —And like I said before, on Tuesday we're headed 'down unda' to Australia to learn the business end of the faire. When I hear myself say that, I just can't believe it. I get Tomas, and the faire in Australia, and Dall and Emily back as my friends... All my dreams are coming true!"

Jaelle had several sarcastic remarks on the tip of her tongue, but she was all choked up with tears and couldn't speak.

Finally, Amber caught a clue and showed some sympathy for an old friend who had been heartbroken by the love of her life.

"Listen to me, going on about how happy Tomas and

I are. How are you doing? I can't believe you and John stayed together these past seven years only to break up right before your wedding. Really, how are you doing?"

Jaelle sniffled.

"Thanks for shutting up about you and Tomas. Now shut up about me and John." She laughed a little. An awkward laugh.

But it was going to be okay.

Amber laughed a little too, in empathy, which was the desired effect.

"Sorry. That was really stupid of me. All of it. What kind of friend am I?"

Jaelle heaved a heavy sigh and wiped her tears away with another part of her T-shirt, blew her nose again, then took it off and threw it in the washing machine. Casting about for something else to put on while it was in there, she found a weird tunic thing in the box and put that on. At least it was clean.

"No, I get it. And I'm really happy for you and Tomas. You're both great people, and I know how in love you are. And I'm one of the few who know why you were apart these past seven years. I know you never really broke up. I know Tomas disappeared from your life to protect you from the heartbreak of having your fourth born son slave for the druids as a time traveler. I know Tomas didn't know that until his parents told him on his eighteenth birthday. But Amber, Dall and Emily thought they were doing the right thing, you know, not telling him until then. You do know that, right? Because I don't hate them or John's parents, and you shouldn't either."

Amber made a humming noise that meant don't worry.

"I don't hate them. I know it's not their fault. He told me the story about their ancestor with a gambling problem who became beholden to a druid and basically sold his descendants into slavery — uh oh, I hope I'm not saying something you don't already know." Amber laughed her exaggerated nervous laugh.

Jaelle opened another beer and took a big swig. It soothed her throat, which was sore from crying.

"Yeah, that story. I bet it was a lot easier for you to believe than it was for me, since you got to go back in time and everything. I'm having trouble believing your story, and I've known the gambling story for seven years now."

Jaelle laughed again, and this time there was actually joy in it.

"Heh," said Amber, "I wouldn't believe my story if I hadn't lived it, so I know what you mean. But here we are talking about me again. I really want to know if you're okay, and if there's anything I can do to help you. I'm not even above going over and giving John a piece of my mind, if that will help..."

Jaelle talked with Amber a while longer about the guys they'd hung out with back when they were all in their teens.

While she did, she drank two more beers and dug through John's boxes. They held mostly junk, but a round iron object caught her attention. She dug for it through a bunch of other stuff.

Wow. It looked like one of the helmets the Roman

soldiers wore in the old drawings in some of the history books in the library.

"What was that?" Amber asked.

"Oh sorry. I told you John let me keep his house after he broke off our engagement, right?"

"Yeah, you did. And you have to admit, that was really nice of him. Most guys wouldn't even let you keep the ring."

Jaelle snorted a laugh and sloshed the beer she was drinking.

"It's not like he's still paying the rent. I'm paying it on my own, when we had planned on splitting it or him paying most of it with the money from the family antique business. No, it wasn't nice of him. Not really. It was more like he couldn't be bothered to move all this junk out and left it to me to deal with. Anyway, I'm going through the boxes, and I found one thing that is really cool. Here, I'll take a picture of it."

Jaelle texted it to Amber and finished her beer. She went to the bag to get another one, but there weren't any left. Feh.

Amber sounded impressed.

"Wow, that is cool."

Oh yeah, the helmet.

"Isn't it? Here, I'm going into video chat to try it on so you can see."

Amber laughed.

"Okay."

As soon as she switched into video chat, Jaelle marveled at her friend's appearance for a moment.

Amber had been on this Goth chick kick for the last few years. It had saddened Jaelle whenever Amber went into video chat to show her the dig she had been working in Mexico. Big skull earrings. White makeup that didn't look good on her olive skin. Black lipstick and black eye makeup.

But now that her friend had married the love of her life, the only thing still the same was Amber's gorgeous long black hair. Well, and the amber colored eyes her parents had named her for. She looked normal now, and happy.

After only a moment of pondering this, Jaelle's excitement at finding the helmet resumed. She set the phone down and ran around in front of the camera.

"Are you watching? I can't tell."

"Yeah, I can see you."

Jaelle held the helmet up over her head.

"Here goes."

FOUR

Breth swam far enough north of the barbarian fort and wall that he felt safe on land, then climbed up onto the rocky shore and shook out his short hair. He found a spot where the early morning sun hit the rocks and sat down to let it dry him — which shouldn't take long, as apart from the woad designs, he was wearing only his boots and the sword sheathed on his back.

Yesterday morning at sunrise, the druids of his clan had ritually painted his entire body with woad-dyed goose grease patterns before he went scouting their people's greatest enemy, the imposters. Even after his swim, the grease still clung to his skin in most places, and while the sun dried him, he amused himself by rippling his muscles and watching a horse dance on his calf.

Once his skin was dry, he started through the woods toward home. His heavy leather boots squished with each step, but overall he was warm and comfortable.

He was walking and not quite whistling but enjoying himself and the accomplishment of having scouted out the fort — when he tripped over something.

He gasped.

That something was a person.

A female person.

Nevertheless, she was a stranger, and even more so, a stranger wearing a Roman helmet. So he drew his sword and trained it on her.

But then she astonished him.

Before he could say anything, she was lighting into him with words in his own language. But what rendered him speechless was that he had never heard a woman use the particular words she was using. Quite graphic words.

While he stood there marveling at this, he wondered.

Her accent, tone, and slang were identical to his, as if the two of them had grown up together.

But he had never seen her before, nor heard anyone like her spoken about.

It was odd to the point of being impossible. Especially the part about her wearing a barbarian helmet. And aside from being unfamiliar to him, she was outright strange anyway. Her hair was shorter than any woman's he had ever seen: only down to her shoulders. She had on tight blue leggings instead of a skirt. And in addition to the helmet, she was wearing an invader's tunic.

Perhaps she was some savage's consort. Some savage who had amused himself by cutting off most of her hair...

Shockingly, the thought of anyone harming her upset him, so he abandoned it.

But what was she doing over here on this side of the wall? This strange woman was wearing enemy clothing and had come into Pictland by herself.

Was she a spy?

Or worse, a charming female assassin?

As she continued to chew him out, he studied her, telling himself he had to keep her at arm's length. Well, he would until he knew more about her. She seemed so... innocent. Guileless. Passionate. Full of a vibrancy absent from all the women he had ever known, this one had a story to tell, and he wanted to hear it.

There must be an innocuous explanation for her attire, surely, because Breth wanted to know more about her. He knew he ought to throw her over his shoulder and run with her to the wall and pitch her over. But despite himself, he was fascinated.

The fact that a woman he had never met before in his life was uncharacteristically furious at him didn't hurt his attraction for her at all. Not in the least. Unlike any other woman he had known — including his mother — she was letting him know she was angry at him.

Women just didn't do that.

Not so you could hear them.

Not on purpose.

She took the helmet off and tossed it on the ground, where it make a *thunk* noise that startled her, making her jump. And all the while, she berated him, trying to pass off her startled leap as a hop toward him and failing in a most attractive way.

Her hands were planted firmly on her hips when

they weren't brushing her hair out of her face, her deep brown eyes were full of fire, she kept tossing her curly brown hair out of her way but it kept flopping into her face anyway and making her cheeks red in a pretty way, and her angry mouth ran the whole time.

"Why don't you watch where you're going? You could have killed me with your clumsy feet. What kind of person kicks a woman in the head when she's lying in the middle of the road..."

At this point, she looked all around, plainly surprised to find herself in the forest on his side of the wall. But she didn't let that stop her vicious verbalism.

"Well you could have killed me, you know. You really need to be more careful. Didn't your mother teach you to be careful around other people? Lack of consideration is not a good trait in a person..."

While she nagged at him, Breth studied this odd stranger more closely, looking for clues that would tell him where she came from and what she was up to.

She was a bit too well-fed for his liking. The daughter of someone prosperous, no doubt. Certainly not from Pictland, or he would have seen her before.

She was afraid, judging by the way she never looked at him.

Yet she was curious about him, because her eyes kept trying to study him, and then she would make them look away. She would gulp when she made herself look away.

But he admired her refusal to cower. He marveled at it. And so he let her berate him. It wasn't costing him anything, not with no one around who could tease him about it later.

He wanted to ask her how she knew his language, but she wasn't letting him get a word in edgewise, still covering her fear by going on and on about how careless he was and how his mother hadn't raised him correctly.

It was hard not to laugh, she was so helpless and yet so ferocious.

Like a kitten.

But an extraordinary kitten.

Her fingernails were long and clean, her hands so smooth as she gestured at him in anger that he longed to find out what it felt like to hold someone's hand who had never worked in the fields. She wasn't a beauty, but her features were miraculously unscarred by weather. If he hadn't heard her speak with such worldly experience, he would have thought her barely of fertile age.

She must have lived inside somewhere safe and warm all her life. Yes, perhaps she was even nobly born, but of what people it was difficult to surmise. She had the eyes and skin of the migrant Jews, but also the hands of the Saxons, the battle stance of the fierce Norse, and the temper of the red-headed Gaels.

She was endowed well enough in all the right places...

What was he thinking? His dear Caitlin was barely nine moon cycles dead. He should mourn her a bit longer before...

He smacked himself in the back of the head and then tried to pass it off as scratching under his hair.

He had to keep control of himself, which meant his thoughts as well.

Perhaps she was the concubine of the barbarian chieftain, being a lady and all. But she sure didn't speak or act like a lady, let alone one who had run away from her captors.

He sniffed, unable to believe what he smelled, now that he was close to her. The better to study her was all.

Was that ale on her breath?

And would she ever run out of breath to scold him with?

"Well don't you stand there gawking, show me to the nearest town. And tell me where in Heaven's name we are. Quit being so impertinent and start being useful, if you want to make it up to me for kicking me in the head like a dolt so that I don't take you to court and... That's weird. I can't think of the word I want there. It's when you... You get a... Well never mind. You know what I mean..."

Biting his cheeks to keep from making her realize her tirade was more comical than frightening, he sheathed his sword on his back and raised his hands up in an ancient sign of peaceful surrender.

"I refuse to take you to the nearest town, but I'm headed to where my clan is stationed. Will that suffice, kitten?"

On hearing the words 'clan is stationed,' she turned every which way with such a forlorn look on her face that he almost felt sorry for her, but not quite. After all, she wore the tunic and helmet of the savages who had killed his Caitlin.

She had pluck, though. Her eyes finally rested on him, but with a quizzical look that wasn't as forlorn as a moment ago. The effect was slightly ruined by the blush that rose in every visible bit of her skin, but she was resolved to be in command. It was so unlike anything he'd seen before in a woman that he couldn't help admiring her.

"Very well, take me to your village, then. You have me at a disadvantage. I can't remember how I got here or even where here is, but I have to assume I'm in Scotland, since you speak of clans and are wearing that ridiculous blue war paint. Don't you know it was the Picts who painted themselves blue with woad? That was two thousand years ago. Really, I would think someone who lives here ought to know that. It's the first thing you learn when you read any ancient Scottish history at all. Of course, most of the history was written by the Romans. They were partial to their own side of the story, but a recent retranslation says it wasn't even woad but crushed blue glass that the Picts rubbed into their skin and scarred themselves with..."

She kept going on.

And on.

And on.

He wondered if she was daft. That was the only explanation for the crazy things she was saying.

Growing weary of her endless jibber jabber, he turned and started walking toward his clan.

"I'll be going now."

She spoke much longer than he thought she would before she realized how helpless she was and started following him with careless running steps which scattered rocks and pieces of bark and twigs in their clumsiness.

Not only was she a kitten, but a house kitten at that. No experience with the outdoors.

At long last, Breth allowed himself to smile.

FIVE

Marcus Androlocles Severus, a distant cousin of Emperor Hadrian, got out of the too-small bath and waited impatiently while two female slaves dressed him in his white woolen toga, wrapping it around his corpulent body and then carefully draping it over one of his shoulders and fastening it with a brooch.

Looking in the inadequate burnished bronze mirror, he had one of the female slaves comb and oil his long curly brown hair while the other one trimmed and buffed his fingernails and toenails, then fitted his golden sandals to his feet.

On his own, he donned all of his gold chains and polished his jeweled rings before he left his chambers to inspect his fort with the kind of care expected of him by the emperor — may he live forever and be worshipped in the manner he deserved.

Ugh. When would he be done with this remote

island full of savages and return to the mainland, where there were vineyards and wineries and so much more of the finer things in life? Unlike here. Here was just grass and trees and stony mountainous ground unsuitable for farming.

He grinned as he ran his finger over the top of the armory cabinet, certain he would find dust that needed cleaning — but he was disappointed.

He could at least find mirth in the fact that he, and his own, had deprived the local savages of the arable land to the south, having driven them north of this wall his fort's men guarded.

He saw a clump of soldiers at their ease in the next room. That wouldn't do at all.

"You there!"

They looked up at him but didn't move.

What impertinence! He was going to...

Oh wait. They were that new squadron who had arrived just this morning, fresh off the ship and unaware of how he wanted things done here.

He indulged himself in his most patient smile. He would educate them.

"Yes, you! All of you! Get up and get over here."

They got up, but they only started walking over.

He threw his arms up in a dramatic gesture of impatience and strength. Educating them might prove too difficult. Maybe it would be better to make examples of them. The other men were well-educated by now to what he preferred, but a reminder now and then couldn't hurt. Couldn't hurt him or his reputation, that was.

Well, on second thought, he didn't want to work up a sweat so soon after he had just bathed and been dressed. He would try one more time to educate them.

"Run over here as if your lives depended on it, because they do!"

Seeing sense at last, the new squadron did indeed run over the rest of the way, and when they got there, they properly bowed.

Oh well. Educating them hadn't been too difficult after all. But now that they were here, they needed a task.

Inspiration struck.

"Follow me."

He marched them outside into a corner of the court-yard, where some local Picts he had enslaved were erecting another lookout tower. He turned to his new squadron.

"You lot will take over construction here. And see to it that these Picts haul those bricks for you from that pile over there to a new pile right here where you can reach them. Supervise them one-on-one. You can't be too guarded against these savages. Given an instant's opportunity, they'll slit your throat."

The squadron nodded and looked over the construction site, angling for a way to get up and resume the work as they discussed the task at hand amongst themselves.

"I know masonry, I'll go up."

"I do as well. Anyone else?"

"No? Well then the rest of you choose a savage each and supervise them carrying the bricks over."

One of them addressed Marcus.

"Even with that large pile moved over here, there won't be enough bricks. What then?"

Perhaps this was getting too difficult after all. Longing to get back to his chamber in the innermost sanctum of the fort where he could lounge on his padded chair and be massaged by his female slaves while being served all the delicacies that were to be had in this drab land, Marcus huffed an exaggerated huff and rolled his eyes in his most impatient way, putting his hand over the side of his face.

"Then we'll have the slaves make more bricks, obviously."

Meanwhile, the Picts were putting down their masonry tools and descending the scaffolding they had erected. Just as the last one's foot touched the stone floor of the courtyard and the two masons among his new squadron prepared to go up, the scaffolding rattled and shook.

One of the men in his new squadron pushed Marcus down onto the cold stone of the courtyard floor.

How dare he!

But before Marcus could open his mouth to insist that the man be flogged fifty times with the lash to his bare back and then hung by the neck until dead, too large heavy clay pots of mortar hit the paving stones where Marcus had been standing a moment before. The clay pots shattered, and the mortar flew everywhere, splattering gobs in his freshly oiled hair and on his freshly washed face and undyed wool toga.

Feeling indignant at having been pushed to the

ground nevertheless, Marcus got up without even dusting himself off or flinging the mortar off of him. He pointed to the slave who had gotten off the scaffolding last and spoke to the soldiers of the new squadron who had just come out here with him.

"Don't just stand around. Find a rope and hang him from the scaffolding until he is dead. And then make sure these other slaves finish this work here, cleaning this up and hauling all those bricks over here."

He waited while this commenced and then looked up at the two who had climbed the scaffolding.

"Quit gawking and resume building this tower!"

They hopped to it.

Satisfied, Marcus headed back to his chamber with an anticipatory grin. It appeared he was in need of another bath.

SIX

Cradling the helmet in her arm as if it were a baby, Jaelle frantically ran through the forest to catch up with the naked Pict.

Jumping Jehoshaphat!

She had time traveled. Without John. Well, with the help of his helmet. But she didn't need John in order to time travel! She had done it anyway, had gone all the way back to the time of the Celts. And she had met one who was a Pict.

This.

Was.

Awesome!

And to top it all off, the helmet had done some sort of magic on her and made her able to speak so that the Pict understood. And she understood what that gorgeous man said, too. She hoped she would remember his language after she returned home, because no one in her time knew Pictish. It was a lost language, only alluded to in the carvings of a few surviving stones.

But arg!

She flushed all over in embarrassment, glad the Pict had rushed on ahead of her and couldn't see her right now.

Why had her mouth run on and on at him as if he were a man she had met in her own time at the museum, spouting off all her bookish knowledge and acting like she was in control when she obviously was not?

Well, she knew why.

Because the Pict was naked!

In the buff.

Wearing nothing but woad and weapons.

As she ran and thought about it, she gradually realized that yelling like that had been a form of defense. Instinctively, she had tried to give the incredibly toned and strong man so much to think about that the idea of taking her by force didn't even occur to him. She could see that now.

So even as she ran after him, she wondered at the wisdom of doing so. Men from this time were not known for their chivalry.

But he had been decent so far.

And he was a known commodity. The next man she met might not be so nice. And if she was with this first man, he might stand up for her against the others.

Anyway, she had the helmet. If things got scary, she would just put it on and go home.

Biting her tongue every time it tried to go off on the man who rushed on ahead of her, she followed him like that for a while, never quite catching up so that she wouldn't have to look at him. Well, who was she kidding? So that he wouldn't catch her looking at him and see just how flustered it made her that he wasn't wearing any clothes.

She had read about the Picts in the Roman history books, of course. She had known intellectually that the Romans had fought naked warriors painted in blue woad. But books hadn't come close to preparing her for naked flesh and blood right in front of her eyes.

Huffing a bit for breath because he walked so fast and had such long legs that were shapely and covered in all this blue stuff and fascinating...

Well, she felt like she really had to stop and speak to him.

"Please tell me we're almost there and I can sit down soon."

He stopped, turned around, and laughed. But it wasn't a mocking laugh. And it wasn't unkind, just amused. His face crinkled up in an attractive way when he laughed. Even from this far away, it affected his whole countenance and made him not scary at all but rather someone she would like to get to know...

Well that was a stupid thought.

Of course she wouldn't be here long enough to get to know anybody.

Right, but she could enjoy him a little bit. He seemed

like that sort of person. Wise. And surprisingly kind and understanding, for a walking killing machine. Her eyes kept staring at his magnificently naked body with nary an ounce of fat on it and every part exquisite.

She knew she should get moving. Should say something. But she was spellbound. He was that much eye candy.

But then the laughter stopped abruptly and he became once more the scary man, scowling at her and throwing his hand back the way they had come.

"You shouldn't come home with me, now that I think about it. You're dressed like one of those invaders who are bent on driving my people off our land. We're at war with them, and of course you know that. I'm not sure what you're doing here. Perhaps if you can give me a good explanation, then I will bring you with me and vouch for you. But I have to warn you I've just about resolved against it."

Desperate for him not to leave her here alone, Jaelle pleaded with him with her eyes and scrunched her lips up over on one side of her face to show him she was thinking.

And she was.

On the one hand, she was super curious about this man's home. Not much was known about the Picts at all. If she could know even a little bit about how they lived and was able to document it with archaeological evidence, she would be famous and employed the rest of her life, regardless of any lack of official schooling. It was the kind of break she had been dreaming of her whole life.

But on the other hand, this man looked fierce. Even without the sword on his back — which she had no doubt he knew how to use like it was an extension of his arm — he looked like he could kill a bear and skin it in the space of five minutes — with his bare hands. He was a hundred percent human but fully confident in the wild just like an animal.

He was fearsome — and so impressive she couldn't help staring...

Anyway, the point was that if he was a veritable killing machine, probably the rest of his people were too — even the women. It was a dangerous place for her to go.

But she had the opportunity of a lifetime, and she would be an idiot not to take a chance on it. After all, she did have a guaranteed mode of escape.

Still cradling the helmet, Jaelle opened her mouth to promise she wouldn't cause him any trouble. To entreat him to take her along.

But before she got the chance, an arrow whizzed past where the two of them stood gabbing. It came from behind them and lodged itself in a nearby tree.

Both at the same time, she and the Pict took off running toward the trees several feet in front of them on the other side of the small clearing. In hindsight, it seemed stupid to have stopped here, out in the open and exposed this way.

Once they were deep enough into the woods where pursuit had to happen single file, they both chose a deep clump of trees to hide in so that they couldn't be surrounded. The Pict drew the sword he carried on his back and wildly looked around for the most defensible place.

They decided on the same spot and ran there together, each glancing in appreciation at the other's knowledge of tactics. Because he was armed and she wasn't — or maybe because she was a woman, it was hard to tell — he put her behind him and stayed behind the cover they'd found, waiting for the people who had shot at them to follow into their ambush.

Jaelle held the helmet above her head, ready to put it on at any moment.

The wait wasn't long.

A Roman soldier wearing a similar helmet, a similar tunic, and leather armor came crashing through the branches of the nearby trees, looking every which way but where she and the Pict waited.

After putting this attacker down in a second, the Pict moved on to the next.

The Roman lay in front of Jaelle, clutching at his side and screaming in agony.

But she wasn't looking at him. Her eyes were fixed a few feet deeper into the woods. The Roman had dropped his sword, and it was now lying where she could reach it. After a quick glance at the Pict, she was satisfied that he would block the attackers from coming in here for a few moments at least, time enough for her to go grab the sword.

As she dashed past the fallen Roman, she felt his grip on her ankle.

Using her training and experience, she stepped into the grip. As she expected, it loosened, and she was able to kick her way free.

But in so doing, she dropped the helmet.

It hit the man in his injured side, and he cried out anew.

Now she stood between the sword and the helmet, with enemies approaching. Quickly deciding she wouldn't have time to put the helmet on but that the sword would serve her well, she bent over and picked it up, then pivoted around to put it in front of her protectively.

Just in time, too.

The next fighter was proving more of a challenge to the Pict.

Jaelle moved over to the Pict's non-sword-arm side and lent her assistance.

Together, they downed the second man.

And the third.

And the fourth.

The rest retreated.

Jaelle picked up the helmet and once again cradled it in her left arm, keeping the sword ready in her right hand and watching the entrance as the Pict searched the men who were down.

She spoke to his back as he did so, careful to stand clear. She had been lucky one time, but she didn't want to tempt these men. They were down, but not out.

"I'm Jaelle Penzag, by the way. I know you're wondering where I'm from, and the best I can tell you is my people come from Israel. That is my true home, and we will all return there someday, when our messiah king comes. For now, we've been scattered to the four corners of the world. We're everywhere. It's nice to meet you. What are you looking for?"

SEVEN

Touched by Jaelle's story of the woes of her people, Breth stood from his search of the invading soldiers and glanced around at them significantly.

"We shouldn't talk here, and anyway, the other men will come back to gather up the fallen. Follow me."

He hadn't consciously made the decision to do so, but he was leading her toward home. She had saved his life, and so now he trusted her. It was that simple.

They made their way out through the one opening in the trees and then went around the large thicket and back into the forest. This wasn't the fastest way home, but it was the safest, under the cover of trees the whole way.

Once he was confident they weren't being followed by the barbarians, he stopped and removed from the bag the belt and scabbard he had acquired for her. And another leather bag for her helmet, which she seemed to be intent on keeping, she cradled it so tightly in her arm.

"Here, these should help."

She stepped up to him and held out her hands to accept his gift, but then she looked up into his eyes and he was caught staring into hers for an amount of time that should have been awkward between strangers. But they no longer were strangers. Now they were fighting companions. Allies.

Her eyes were dark and mysterious and utterly captivating. Seeing that she was looking at him in much the same regard, he crinkled his nose in a conspiratorial smile.

She put the belt on and sheathed her new Roman sword, bagged the helmet and tucked the mouth of the bag under the belt, then looked up at him expectantly.

Oh yeah.

"I'm Breth, and my people have lived here for many generations. It was long ago we came here from over the sea. This is our home, and we are here. Your story makes me appreciate that more, so thank you for the reminder."

She slowly nodded once, with sadness in her eyes.

It stirred him, the deep emotion she was showing...

But they needed to get moving, so he gestured ahead of him and started walking before he spoke, pleased that she fell in easily by his side.

"Why such sadness? At hearing this from me, why are you sadder than when you told me the plight of your own people?"

With her eyes cast faraway over the highland mountains, she spoke more readily. It made him grin, seeing how he affected her.

"Oh, it's nothing. Just some dirt in my eyes. Aren't you cold without any clothes on? You could've taken the clothes off of those men back there and had something to wear instead of going about buck naked like that. You've got to be cold. I would be cold — not that I would go about naked, so don't get any ideas."

He laughed.

"Are you kidding? This is so liberating. Maybe you should try it."

She wrinkled her brow at him, but even so she was looking him over more openly now than she had before.

"No, I'm not kidding. Not about me going naked, nor you. Why do you have to do that?"

He reached out and caught a branch before it hit her in the face. He was quite enjoying this more tentative and less angry side of her. Still, he wasn't ready to tell her the whole truth. If she could sidestep questions, then so could he.

"Well, if I wore clothes, then you couldn't admire the druids' handiwork on me, now could you?"

When she looked at him incredulously, he flexed his biceps and made the rabbit jump, then manipulated the muscles in his chest and made the water fall down the rapids.

Her mouth hung open, and she looked up at him with wide eyes, pretty in the lacy shade of the trees.

"Do they all move like that?"

He smiled, quite pleased that she was impressed.

"Aye, they do." One by one, he demonstrated them all

for her staring eyes — becoming quite affected himself in the process.

She blushed at this and turned away and started walking once more in the direction they had been headed, grabbing the branches and throwing them out of her way as she did so.

Hm.

He didn't know too much about the Jewish people, but right now, he would wager they didn't use ritual body painting.

He had her off balance, and he would press the advantage and get some answers. He quickly caught up with her and held his hands out to clear a path for her as he walked beside her.

"What did all that stuff mean, what you said to me when you were angry? Who's talking about my people that way? What makes them think our druids would scar the people with glass? That's such an unnatural idea. The druids would never do that. Their power comes from the forces of nature." Oops. Careful.

But she gave no sign of noticing his slip of the tongue. Caught up in his question, she scrunched up her mouth and smiled at the same time, making her look sheepish, but also like she was holding a secret close. Yes, he thought so.

"No one important said those things. And no one close enough to matter. These people are far, far away, and they sit at their ease, speculating on what's going on in another part of the world altogether. You needn't worry about them. They cannot affect you."

Yes, she was evading his question. He walked on in silence for a few moments, then tried a different tactic for his interrogation. A trick question that would give him information he wasn't ostensibly asking for. If she agreed with him suddenly and eagerly, then he would know she was lying for sure.

"How could you possibly have spoken to people so far away? You aren't old enough to have traveled around the world — unless you were born over there and only just arrived here?"

But her reaction surprised him.

She showed an odd sort of confidence, pulling her chin in quickly while smiling with only one side of her mouth. It was most unfeminine. And most attractive because of this. Really, everything about her was fresh and new and ... intriguing.

"Oh no, I haven't spoken to them. Are you kidding? No, I'm nobody important enough to have spoken to them. I've only read their ... pictures."

Now he was the one hitting the branches out of their way abruptly, instead of just pushing them aside. She was being deliberately obtuse. She was hiding something. It made him fight his attraction to her, and a sense of disappointment settled on him. He still trusted her with his life, but his suspicion that she was here to spy on him was growing. He didn't think she was spying for the invaders, but it had to be for someone. The Gaels, perhaps.

"How did you travel so far to read their pictures?"

She was quiet for a moment, perhaps thinking up a lie to tell him.

"Yeah, that's right. They say you make your pictures on large immovable stones. How do I explain this? Um ... Some people draw their picture stories on small stone tablets that can be borrowed and taken great distances to be read by others. And some communicate by drawing on hides, or rolls of plant matter similar to hides."

He chewed on that while they found a place to cross a small stream, then jumped from rock to rock until he reached the far bank.

Quite far ahead of her and calling back over his shoulder now that they were well away from the imposters, he led the way up a path hidden in the heather between the trees of the forest.

"How do these people communicate with things that move from place to place? Carvings tell the story of the place where we carve them. They wouldn't make sense anyplace else."

She finished jumping from the last stone and landed with a scattering of the small rocks on the stream bank, then ran up to him.

"Well, their pictures tell different stories. My own people's pictures tell the stories of all the things our God has done for us, and... Actually, now that I think about it, many people's stories are mostly about what they believe in."

Now at the top of the riverbank, the path changed direction, following the stream's gulley. He paused there, giving her a chance to catch up — and to confess.

"And yet you say others have drawn my people's stories. Why would they do this, and how do they know about us? And by the way, why do you have the clothing and helmet of the imposters?"

She sighed as she picked her way over a haphazard rock pile in the path.

"People all over the world know about you Picts because of the Romans who have traveled here. I've seen some of the pictures they've drawn of your naked bodies decorated with woad, so I knew to expect it. Even so, the reality is rather..." She looked away from him, down the path, blushing. "...disturbing. And as to your 'by the way,' my own clothing suffered an accident, so I grabbed what clothing was available."

This was both maddening and intriguing. She answered his questions satisfactorily, but she was holding back. She was tougher under the pressure of interrogation than he would have expected, given her kitten-like nature. But then again, she was also competent with a sword, something he never saw coming...

As the path veered off to climb a hill, he was mulling this over and trying to decide what it meant when she asked two questions of her own.

"Are we going to your home? And if so, what sort of place is it?"

She was looking at him with such a combination of interest and uncertainty that he had to laugh.

"You mean what sort of home could a painted savage possibly make for himself?"

She tripped over a rock that wasn't there, then closed her eyes and shook her head quickly. And when she spoke, she was stammering.

"I – I – I didn't say that."

He waited until she looked at him and inclined his head forward, raising his eyebrows at her, challenging her to tell him he was wrong. But he kept on leading her toward his home. She was here anyway, and it was better if he kept a potential spy where he knew what she was doing.

"Nay, but you were thinking it. I can see it in your eyes. You find me unsophisticated. You imagine your people more advanced than mine."

She kicked the next rock she came to and sent it skittering along the pathway by the creekside before she took a heavy sigh and looked at him pleadingly.

"That's terrible of me, and I'm sorry. I really don't know the first thing about you or your people, besides whatever I read in other people's drawings. Roman drawings. They are obsessed, but they don't have any respect for you. They call you savages, and I shouldn't have bought into their opinions. I hope you will forgive me my prejudice."

EIGHT

Jaelle wanted to disappear into a puff of smoke and fly away. Breth was right. She had been thinking him inferior to her, his people uncivilized and less advanced. And perhaps that was true of their societies as a whole, but that didn't mean as individuals he or his people were any less knowledgeable or smart.

Her heart beat erratically as she waited for his answer to her apology, giving him her most contrite look and aching inside with embarrassment and shame. And regret. And ... loss?

His face remained stern.

"I thank you for your apology, and I will consider accepting it. To answer your question, we will be there before sunset, so you will soon see for yourself just how primitive our society is. My clan's current home can be seen from the top of this hill we climb."

She lowered her eyebrows in a quizzical look.

"Your current home?"

He continued on leading without turning back this time, and lovely as it was to look at his back, she missed those blue pools of wisdom.

"Aye, it's my clan's turn to man this broch. After a while, we will rotate to our next duty station, and the next clan will take a turn here."

On hearing the word broch, excitement stirred in Jaelle's chest. The ruined brochs were a big mystery in her time, only found in Scotland. No one knew who built them or why. And she was going to see one while people were living there.

But he was so stern, her excitement didn't seem fitting right now. He was displeased with her, and for good reason. She needed to watch her tongue more. Not let it have its way.

She raised her hands up over her head to avoid getting them scratched up by the bushes as she passed through a narrow space along the path.

"I suppose that makes sense," was all she said, trying like mad not to say anything else awful. And then they crested this little hill and she felt her jaw drop and air rush into her mouth as she stared at the broch on top of the next hill.

It must have been fifty feet wide and five stories tall.

She felt startled because the men going about their business up and down the hill were all wearing breeks — knee-length trousers. She expected men in Scotland to be wearing kilts, but she knew that was silly. She knew the Picts wouldn't wrap their plaid blankets around them as clothing until much later, when they missed this time of independence, before they joined forces with the Gaels. But it was odd to be in Scotland and not see kilts.

She didn't miss them terribly much though.

Because in the field between the two hills were warriors at fighter practice.

And all the fighters were naked.

Like Breth.

Truly, it was difficult to not stare.

Breth's voice woke her up from her stupor.

"Are you going to stand there all day, or are you coming?"

Seeing that his face was still stern, she shook her head quickly to clear it.

"Yeah, sorry. The brochs were in the drawings I saw, of course, but I never expected them to be so big. They just looked like piles of ... well, they didn't look so big, and I just had to ... well..."

At this he smiled the tiniest bit.

But it wasn't a friendly smile.

Jaelle had the impulse to take out the helmet and go home this instant. Things were awkward between her and Breth now, not like before all the talking they'd done. She didn't think he would hurt her, though. She had saved his life, after all.

Anyway, how could she pass up the opportunity to see inside a standing broch, let alone one that was occupied?

They walked the rest of the way in silence between the two of them, with pale children running about all around them and naked pale people practice-fighting on the mashed-down grass under the cloudy sky. None of these other fighters were decorated with woad.

They called out greetings.

Well, the people greeted Breth, and Jaelle tried her hardest not to stare at them.

They didn't return the favor though. They were staring at her openly. And she supposed with good reason, seeing as how she was wearing a Roman tunic and anachronistic blue jeans.

But Breth was her insurance policy. They did stare at her, but then they looked at him and he looked at them as if to tell them 'She's under my protection.' It made her feel warm and fuzzy inside, even though he didn't even introduce her.

They honored this, and it wasn't even a close thing. She didn't feel threatened.

But she didn't dare wander far from him.

Things were still awkward between her and him, though. The bounce of the helmet in its bag against her rear end was more reassuring than ever.

Aside from the smoke coming out through its thatched roof, the broch resembled a tall stone hill with a tiny wooden door. Inside, she heard goats bleating, cows lowing, and chickens clucking.

Breth knocked.

"It's Breth come home with news."

The door opened, revealing a brown-haired Pictish warrior, brandishing a big sword. Another wooden door stood immediately behind him, and stone walls shut him in on both sides. Invaders would have to fight their way through this small space before entering the broch.

Jaelle looked up. Sure enough, holes in the wooden ceiling provided defenders an opportunity to dump on the invaders before they got in.

This new warrior lowered his sword and laughed, then hugged Breth, looking at Jaelle curiously over Breth's shoulder.

"Welcome home. There was a bit of worry you wouldn't make it, with all the trouble that's started—"

Breth pulled back from the hug and cut off whatever the man was saying, both with words and with a gesture toward her.

"Aye, we saw some trouble of our own. More about that later. For now I want to get our guest settled. Send Deoord up with more suitable clothes for her."

Again, he hadn't introduced her, but at least he had called her a guest. That was encouraging, right?

The guard nodded once in acknowledgment and then stepped out of the little alcove. Breth took her inside and closed the outer door. Only once it was closed did he open the inner door.

Tiny rays of sunlight peeked through the cracks in the ten foot thick stone walls, trying to light the room and failing. Perhaps to make up for this, four small stone enclosures near the center of the room held fires, and their smoke went up through the driftwood ceiling, which must be the floor on the next level.

Down here on the first level, the dirt floor was tightly packed, and Jaelle's feet didn't stir any dust at all as she walked on it. The thirty foot diameter room was full of little lean-to dividers with bedding inside. Chickens scratched all over, and goats were tied to the stone wall.

A few people lingered here, mostly women chatting with each other. They glanced over her way frequently, but in these relatively close quarters they made a point of not staring. At least there was that.

Breth took Jaelle's hand and led her through another door to a stairway between the inner and outer walls. It was only about a foot and a half wide. She guessed there were no fat people at this time in history. Except the Romans. She'd seen actual drawings of them in addition to reading the texts she had described to Breth as pictures.

"Watch your step," he said as he walked up ahead of her slowly and placed her hand on the wall. It was stone and irregular. "The steps are as bumpy as the walls, so be careful."

"Can't we light a torch or something?" She said as pleadingly as she could while trying to keep up with him.

He laughed.

"Your feet and your hands will get the job done without your eyes if you only allow them to, Kitten. Just take your time. We're going up all five floors."

About ready to drop from exhaustion after staying up basically all night and then walking for miles, Jaelle had to take the stairs exceedingly slowly in order to avoid tripping. She looked longingly at the three wooden doors they passed on their way up. Finally, they were at the top, where another wooden door waited.

Breth opened it and gestured her in.

"This is where I sleep, and so do any guests. If anyone woke up in the middle the night and saw a stranger... Well, just understand you're in this room with me for your own protection."

Jaelle looked around. Her eyes had adjusted on the way up, and now she could actually see by the scant sunlight coming through the cracks between the stones that made up the walls. There was only one room up here, and though the first floor was 30 feet across inside the thick walls, the structure tapered almost to a point up here, so that this room was only 8 feet across. Items of clothing and accessories hung from pegs driven into the chinks in the walls. The wooden floor was covered with bedding except for a small hole in the center, where the smoke billowed up from below and exited through the thatch roof.

She was so sleepy she almost didn't care where she was so long as there was bedding, and there was plenty of it here. But self-preservation told her to resist the idea of letting her guard down for the night with a man she just met, gorgeous or not. Hospitable or not. Having fought off Roman attackers with her or not.

At least, not without talking first.

All right. Truth be told, Jaelle's big mouth just took over. It was only later on she rationalized why.

"So I bet you bring a lot of women up here."

This must have caught him off guard, because he laughed the smallest bit, and this time it was friendly.

"Not as many as you might think."

She pushed some of the bedding aside with her foot so that she could walk around the room and get her bearings, but there weren't any other exits. She settled near the door and sat down on what looked like burlap blankets.

"That isn't any kind of answer."

He raised his eyebrows and crossed his arms, leaning on the curved wall on the other side of the door. His face was frank and open now, at least.

"Do I really owe you an answer?"

She lowered her chin in mock dismay, only realizing afterward it was a flirty thing to do — and then doubly shocked at what her mouth said without consulting with her.

"Well I am a woman alone with you in your bedroom. Usually by this point a man and a woman have at least admitted to each other if they're married or not."

He looked deep in her eyes with his blue ones, making the rest of the world disappear until she was drowning in those blue pools of sincerity.

"And are you hoping I'm married ... or not?"

A rush came over her whole body, the kind of exhilaration she felt when she was aboard an airplane taking off.

"A little of each, actually."

That won her an approving grin. Which made her jaw drop in awe. At close range like this, she watched while the blue woad leaves on his face bloomed into flowers and then sprouted berries when his smile grew more intense and happy.

"Why do you hope I am married?"

She looked upward as if imploring God for strength — when really she just needed a break from those eyes or she was going to do something she regretted.

"Let's just say I don't have the highest confidence in men right now. One of you recently disappointed me in a big way, and I don't want that to happen again. The easiest way to avoid it seems to be only hanging out with men I can't have."

He shrugged, his handsome face amused.

"Sorry, can't help you there. I'm ready and available, poor you."

Her face must've shown her shock at his assumption that she would sleep with him, because just as a thin dark-haired man opened the door and came in holding a bundle of clothes, Breth stifled a laugh, slowly shaking his head no as he gestured for the man to hand her the clothes.

"Aw lass, we shall each stay on our own side of the room. There is plenty of space for that. Put on some of our local clothing and then come down one floor and we'll give you something to eat."

With that, Breth grabbed some clothing off the circular wall and the two men went out the door and closed it softly behind them.

Jaelle was torn between using the helmet to go home now while she had privacy — and being curious about what sort of food they would give her. Curiosity won out, so she took off her jeans and the Roman tunic so she could put on one of the dresses from nearly two thousand years ago. Mostly out of modesty, she left her padded bra on, though she did like the way it lifted her.

There were three dresses in the bundle, all knee-length. For tonight she chose a plaid one that resembled the sheath dresses her mother was fond of, except the skirt had side slits for easy mobility and the short sleeves were composed of many small petals. She marveled at how even in the first century AD, five different colors had been woven into the plaid: green, blue, brown, orange, and even a black thread was woven in. After thinking on it for a moment, she realized she had been discrediting the abilities of these people again. This was an island, after all, so the black thread could've been died with ink from a squid.

She found shoes in the bundle as well, handmade of course, and composed entirely of leather. The souls were surprisingly thick and tough.

She fastened the belt and scabbard on over these clothes, but left the sword on top of her jeans. Much more importantly, she once more tucked the mouth of the leather bag with the helmet into the belt.

Salivating, she opened the wooden door and descended carefully in the darkness, knocking when she came to the next wooden door.

After a few moments, Breth opened it. He had scrubbed the woad off his pale face and hair, and he had donned some of those knee-length breeks and a linen shirt. His once again friendly blue eyes were wide — with admiration? — as he looked at her and spoke, this time reverently.

"Come on in and sit down, Jaelle. The food is ready."

He gestured toward a table with three plates of food on it.

She sat down in the nearest chair, trying not to stare at the food with too much fascination. It was a lost cause though. The food smelled good, but it was unlike anything she'd ever seen before. It was a salad of sorts, but with no lettuce and an unfamiliar dressing. Bits of what must be fish had been tossed into it. There wasn't any tableware in evidence.

Breth sat down and poured wine into wooden cups from an earthenware pitcher.

"Go ahead and dig in."

While she was dying to, she just had no idea how. She waited and watched.

Breth shrugged, grabbed at the salad with his fingers, and took several bites before she dared to join him.

The salad was good, if a bit odd — and messy, eating with the fingers. She didn't see any napkins. She stole a glance at Breth.

He was licking the dressing off his fingers between bites when he caught her looking and winked at her. His smile was friendly again, even more friendly than right after their victory in battle.

This was nice, but confusing.

Deoord was seated across from her, and when she looked up into his eyes, they saw inside her in a manner that wouldn't allow her to look away.

She heard Breth talking to Deoord.

"Can you tell anything else about her?"

Deoord continued studying her without blinking.

"I think she's been spirited to our age in order to help defeat the savages who are building that wall to cage us."

What?

How could this man know that just by looking at her? Or did she smell like something from the future? She felt panicky and irrational under the small man's scrutiny, and the urge to smell her underarms for the scent of her deodorant was nearly overpowering. But that was silly, so she tamped it down, her eyes still held in Deoord's gaze.

Although he was staring at her, the small man was still speaking to Breth as if she weren't in the room. Ordinarily, she knew her tongue would call him out for being rude, but somehow his stare had quieted even her tongue's mind of its own. And that was saying something.

Deoord's voice was contemplative.

"Hopefully she can give us an edge against them, being from the future and knowing the past—"

Oh, Lord help us.

Jaelle stood up and did her best to pierce both of their delusions — and bring them both back down to Earth where they would once again speak to her as the mere human she was. It was unsettling, being revered.

"I don't know how you know I'm from the future, and I don't deny that. But although I do know the past more than most people of my time, I know it only in the big picture. The small details — such as who won which individual skirmish at Hadrian's Wall and how — have escaped the historical record, largely because you Picts don't ... draw on parchment the way I was explaining to

Breth before. The Romans do, and so all the records we have of what happened in this time were ... drawn ... by the Romans. I'm sure you won some battles, but those victories are not recorded. What's more, the Romans have a name for this year in relation to all other years in a system of timekeeping that you are not privy to, and so you wouldn't be able to tell me what year it is so that I could reference what little I do know. I'm sorry. I really can't be of much use to you as a sage."

Whereas before there had been noise and shuffling about in a general hubbub from below, all that was now dead silent.

Well, now the whole clan knew. So be it.

Breth smiled at her again in that friendly way she had enjoyed back when it was all she'd seen from him. Now it worried her. Would he be depending on her the way Deoord was trying to?

But with a pained look on his face, he calmly gestured for her to sit down again and waited while she did.

"Jaelle, not only do I accept your apology, I now apologize to you. I doubted you. I knew you weren't a spy from the invaders, but I thought you might be here spying for the Gaels. Howsoever, Deoord is one of our druids I told you about, with supernatural powers derived from the forces of nature. He assures me you are from far in the future and do not mean us any harm. I just hope you'll accept my apology and stay around long enough to see us defeat the barbarians."

It moved Jaelle, seeing this strong warrior who was

obviously the leader of his clan humble himself. And knowing what was in store for his people had her almost in tears.

She opened her mouth to warn him the Romans were going to win.

But Deoord tapped her shin with his foot, causing her to look at him again. Once he had her gaze, he held it with the power of his own and spoke hurriedly.

"I am unsure of when the fae will take her back, Breth."

Say what?

Huh.

So Deoord didn't want Breth to know that some druids had the power of time travel and had crafted things like this Roman helmet in order to facilitate time travel. And Deoord would be a dangerous person to cross.

Tearing her eyes away from the druid and again looking at Breth's pained face, Jaelle stood up again.

"I accept your apology."

Breth's face broke into a grateful relaxed smile that made him more attractive to her than ever. He stood and began to make his way around the table — probably to clasp forearms with her, but maybe to give her a hug.

Almost impossibly weary now, she held out her hand to stay him.

"I was about to head for bed when I suddenly found myself here in your time. On top of that, I'm not accustomed to walking such distances. I fear that if I don't go up to my bed now, I'll go to sleep right here and fall out of the chair. Will you men excuse me?"

Breth gave her a sympathetic grin and spoke apologetically at first, and then more flirty even than she had been earlier.

"I will. But before you go, I just want you to know you look great in that dress."

Deoord turned his mighty gaze upon Breth and glowered.

Undaunted, Breth beamed a smile, first at him, and then back at her.

NINE

Jaelle had to crawl up the steep hard stone stairs on her bare knees, but she made it without falling. When she was back to where she had left her jeans, she again thought of putting the helmet on and leaving. It was the sensible thing to do.

But Breth's handsome smiling face and sparkling blue eyes appeared in her mind unbidden. Well, okay, and his naked woaded body danced before her mind's eye as well. He was magnificent. And he liked her. And now he knew her secret and things were no longer awkward between the two of them.

She wanted to spend as much time with him as she could before she left.

And, you know, she was learning so much about the Pictish people. That knowledge would help her in her work, which was important, you know. Just one more day. Surely that was within reason. She had a few days off before she needed to be at work again.

Having made the decision, she fell onto the bedding and rolled over once to cover herself up. Within seconds, she was fast asleep.

∼

JAELLE WAS HAVING one of those dreams where she knew she was dreaming. She knew because while she had only glanced at most of the broch as she passed through it, now her dream self was exploring it through her memories. Her choice of companion for this puzzled her, but at least there was no more talk of her companion's recent wedding.

At the thought of a wedding, Breth's ruggedly hand-some face and dancing eyes appeared again unbidden. Eh, maybe it wouldn't be so bad if Amber talked about her wedding some more.

Their friend Kelsey was here in the dream too. The three of them were floating up and down the walls of the broch right through the floors, looking around in wonder, glancing at each other from time to time with that amaze-ment in their eyes that Jaelle had tried to share with Breth the day before, when it had fallen flat.

The three of them stopped for a moment on the bottom floor in the middle of the circle of small fires, and Amber hugged Jaelle.

"I'm so glad you're okay. When you put on that helmet and disappeared, we were both worried sick. Looks like you're doing well there though."

Amber let go and Kelsey hugged Jaelle too.

"Has the same amount of time passed there as here, eight hours?"

Jaelle pulled back from Kelsey's hug and wrinkled her brow at her old friends to show her puzzlement.

"Okay, either this is the most realistic dream I've ever had, or you guys are really here with me. But I know I'm dreaming, so that's not it. But you don't seem at all puzzled, so spill. What's going on?"

Amber made a 'this is a big deal' face and looked at their other friend.

"She had better tell you. It's mostly her story. I don't know all the details."

Kelsey covered her mouth with her hand for a moment, smiling at Jaelle with embarrassment.

"Oh I'm so sorry. You don't know about my ability, do you."

Jaelle raised her eyebrows.

"Uh, no, I guess I don't."

Kelsey gestured at some odd straw mats on the dirt floor and shrugged a question at her and Amber, causing all three of them to sit down and try out the odd furniture. Kelsey made a funny face at how uncomfortable it was.

"Well, it's kind of a long story, but you aren't going anywhere until I let you."

It was foolish to do so in a dream, but Jaelle lunged at Kelsey then, determined to remind her friend that unlike some people, Jaelle hadn't quit fighter practice.

Kelsey raised her hands up in front of her in defense for a second, and then broke into laughter.

"Okay, okay! Sorry, bad joke. So here goes. While you spent almost seven happy years with John, I had no idea if Tavish was even alive—"

Jaelle frowned at Kelsey, half in true sorrow for her friend's loss of those seven years she might have been with Tavish, and half in frustration with her for bringing John's name up. Okay, a third of each of those, and a third with indignation at being complained to about it.

"Yeah, that was awful for you, I know. I know I'm lucky I did have those six and a half years with John, but you have Tavish back now, and I think I've lost John forever to another woman, so—"

Kelsey reached out and hugged Jaelle again, shaking her head quickly.

"No, no, no, don't worry about it. That's not where I was going. Just bear with me. I told you this was a long story, and that was just the introduction."

Jaelle gave Kelsey a squeeze and then let her go gently.

"Sorry. Okay, I won't interrupt anymore. Go ahead. I'm dying to hear this."

Kelsey played with a silver ring on her right ring finger. Now that Jaelle looked at it, she noticed the ring was one big Celtic knot made from several thin silver strands. The thing was gorgeous and intricate.

Her friend continued to play with it as she spoke.

"So while I was missing Tavish so much, you know I went to Celtic University. But the part that even I didn't know was the place is run by druids. The same druids who give Tavish his marching orders because of the curse that was put on the MacGregor family generations ago. The curse that made Tavish and Tomas and John's brothers leave me, Amber, Sarah, Lauren, and Ashley for those seven years."

Through John, Jaelle already knew about the curse. He was under it as well, being part of the same MacGregor family as Tavish. It was what allowed him to time travel, and it had made it possible for him to meet the other woman he ran off with, into the past.

But the curse came from an evil sept of druids which had generations ago enslaved the MacGregor family.

And Kelsey was saying she had discovered only recently that the university where she had spent the past seven years studying for a doctorate was run by this evil sept.

How horrible for her.

Jaelle took Kelsey's hand and squeezed it with what she hoped was reassurance.

Kelsey squeezed Jaelle's hand in return and held it, giving her a grateful and sad smile that was close to tears.

"Yeah, but Tavish and I have made our peace with the curse now. Time travel is adequate — well, not so much compensation for the curse as... Well, I guess time travel is our compensation for having to serve the druids." She looked all around them at the broch in awe and wonder some more. "And you have to admit, time travel is pretty diverting. Downright fun, even."

The two of them met eyes.

Jaelle nodded, raising her eyebrows and tossing her eyes in a 'who could pass this up?' way.

"I have to admit, a small part of my disappointment when John broke up with me was over the loss of the time traveling life I thought we would share. But look, I'm time traveling without him. Who knew?"

Kelsey gave her a knowing nod, raising one eyebrow to say 'exactly.'

"Well, I'll cut the story short after all." She held up her right hand, spinning her silver ring with her thumb. "This is my graduation ring from Celtic University. Amber has told you some of the story of how Tavish accidentally took me time traveling and then how we brought her into it, right?"

Jaelle looked at Amber and smiled an apology for getting crabby with her on the phone earlier.

Amber acknowledged it with a nod and by scrunching up her nose playfully.

Jaelle turned back to Kelsey.

"Right, she has. I didn't want to hear it amid all her talk of being back together with Tomas, but she did try to tell me about your adventures together."

Looking amused, Kelsey moved around on the thin straw mat that sat on the cold stone floor. Trying to make herself comfortable and failing, she looked at Jaelle and laughed some more.

"Yeah, well a fourteenth century druid named Brian saw my ring and called me 'Priestess.' That was my first clue the druids were involved with Celtic University. But they're more than just involved. They trained me in all of their ways without my realizing it by making it about folklore end mythology and all the old stories that explained the old artwork and architecture. They guided me into..."

Kelsey sighed heavily.

"There is no easy way to say this, so I'm just gonna blurt it out and hope you don't hate me."

Jaelle's friend choked up, and tears fell down her face, but she struggled through it and kept talking anyway.

"Unbeknownst to me, what I was really doing at Celtic University was... becoming a druid myself—"

Jaelle and Amber both gently caressed Kelsey's back while she cried and kept talking to them. She paused from time to time, taking several deep breaths every few moments to calm her sobbing, but she continued on.

"Being a druid priestess isn't all bad, though. I get to time travel with Tavish, because they think I can handle it. If I didn't have this ability, they probably wouldn't allow it. That would be much less bearable. And the second good thing I've gotten from becoming a druid myself is this ability. As you have probably figured out by now, this isn't just a dream. Amber and I are really here with you, in the dream world. You'll remember all of this when you wake up, and so will we. I can come into the dreams of anyone I've ever touched in real life. I can either share the time with the dreamer— which I always do when I enter a friend's dream—or, I can search through the dreamer's memories while they dream, unaware of me. It's a powerful ability, and I'm so used to having it now that I'm not sure I would give it up in order to not be involved with the druids anymore. But we especially don't think we could ever give up time travel voluntarily, not unless it meant that all the children in our family would be free from serving the druids through time travel for evermore. Maybe then we could give it up. Maybe."

Jaelle waited to see if Kelsey was going to tell more of her fascinating story, but her friend had clammed up. Giving her a sympathetic look, Jaelle gestured up at the broch they had just explored.

"I understand. I can't make myself leave now that I've tasted what it's like to actually live history instead of just reading history. It's dangerous here, and I know I should just put the helmet back on and come home. But now that Breth knows I'm from the future and is no longer afraid I'm spying on him for the Gaels, he's excited to have me here and wants to show me all kinds of things, and—"

Kelsey had woken up out of her funk and was looking at Jaelle with amused eyes.

Jaelle looked over at Amber.

Her other friend was just as amused, and gave her a funny look and three quick raises of her eyebrows.

Jaelle sat up from leaning back on her arms.

"What?"

Amber lightly pushed Jaelle's shoulder.

"Breth, huh?"

Jaelle blushed and looked down. She had been caught crushing on a guy in the middle of this serious discussion about druidic curses on the MacGregor family. When was she going to learn to think before she spoke?

Kelsey tapped Jaelle's knee.

"Mind if I give us a look at your Breth through your memories of your day?"

Jaelle blushed even deeper.

"Okay, but don't say I didn't warn you."

Kelsey gave Jaelle a confused look as the broch dissolved and left them all three standing in the woods where Jaelle had first seen Breth.

And there he was in all his... splendor.

Amber gasped and grabbed both of Jaelle's arms. Without taking her eyes off Breth.

"Oh, I so wouldn't be coming back home."

Jaelle couldn't take her eyes off Breth herself. Miles of pale skin, taut muscles, and woad animal decorations which leapt and ran and even winked when he moved. And blue eyes to match that did just as much whenever they met hers.

But Jaelle heard Kelsey's voice off to the side, and it sounded distracted enough to show that her other friend was also drooling over Breth.

"You have a bad deal in that helmet, with time passing at home while you're here... Did that wolf just wink? ...Was it always like that for John? When you were together, would he be gone for long periods of time while he was in the past? Oh my gosh, that waterfall on his chest is flowing! And those blue eyes, whoa! Anyway, no time at all passes for me in the present while Tavish is in the past without me. And I only time travel along with him, never by myself, so when I get back home, it's the same instant I left. That's how I can keep my job."

Jaelle took her concentration off of her memory in order to answer her friend.

To her surprise, the memory sped up, just playing highlights of her and Breth's day.

Amber and Kelsey both squealed in delight at the part where Breth moved all of his muscles and deliberately made the woad illustrations animate for Jaelle's amusement.

Jaelle couldn't bring herself to answer Kelsey's question until all the highlights of the whole day had played out and the three of them are once more seated inside the broch — this time at the fourth floor table where she and Breth and Deoord had eaten their fish salads.

"Having just turned twenty five, John was only starting to time travel when we broke up. And no, he wasn't gone for long periods of time, only a few hours each time. But obviously on the other end he was gone for months. Long enough to meet another woman. And fall in love with her. And choose her over me."

Amber and Kelsey scooted their chairs down the table on either side of Jaelle and put their arms around her, hugging her tight while she cried.

In record time she remembered this was a dream, though, and pulled herself together.

There was something else she remembered.

"Amber, will you do me a big favor?"

Her friend nodded quickly.

"You know I will."

Jaelle recalled — and so Kelsey replayed — how earnest Deoord had looked when he said she would be a help to them because of her knowledge of history. And how disappointed he had looked when she disavowed him of that idea.

She looked pleadingly at Amber.

"I don't know what you have going on in the morning, but I hope you can get online wherever you are. Because I want you to look up the few brochs whose remains are close to Hadrian's Wall and tell me everything you can find out about any battles which took place near them while the wall was still being built."

TEN

Marcus sat comfortably at the table in his quarters with his four generals, talking over his rough map of the local area. He had managed to cobble it together based on the reports of all the scouts they had sent out these past few years. Four scouts had reported in just this morning, and he expected one more.

Female slaves refilled Marcus and the generals' wine goblets, took away their empty breakfast plates, and placed before them new plates with fruit and cheese.

Finally, the last scout was ushered in and prostrated himself face down on the dirt floor at Marcus's feet.

Marcus snapped off a sprig full of grapes from the plate nearest him and concentrated on finding the best ones while he spoke to the scout. He hated it when he popped a sour grape in his mouth, or a wrinkled one. Couldn't be too careful.

"Go on then, give us your report. Don't just dawdle there."

The scout's voice came out high-pitched, which wasn't surprising, seeing as how he was only nine years old.

Marcus used to send out grown men as scouts, but he had decided that was wasteful. Far too many of them never returned. Child scouts were much more successful — either because they were so small and innocent that the enemy ignored them and they didn't die while scouting, or because they missed their mothers and were more motivated to return. Marcus didn't really care which it was, so long as they kept returning. And reporting.

The child piped up in his squeaky voice.

"As you requested, I went as far north as I could in one day. I went by the rock hill and over six more hills, but I didn't find any more rock hills full of savages. In the one hill of rocks there are sixty seven savages, best as I could count in the time I was there. Thirty six of these are grown men, twenty three are grown women, and the rest are children my size and smaller. During the day they practice warfare and at night they all sleep inside the rock hill."

Marcus licked the grape juice off his fingers, dipped them in a finger bowl, and dried them with a cloth napkin that had his name embroidered on it before he turned his attention to the cheese tray. Oh good, there was still some of that great Camembert left.

He spoke to the scout out of the corner of his mouth

while he gobbled it, looking over the rest of the cheese selection and swirling his wine in his goblet.

"This is unacceptable. There must be another rock hill closer inland. You just aren't finding it. If I have explained it to you once, I have explained it a thousand times. The rock hills line the coast almost impenetrably to the north, so why should it be any different here along our wall? You will go back immediately. Comb back and forth more carefully this time along the hillsides. Climb the mountain beyond and see what sort of view it can give you of the area. You will find the next rock hill before you come back here."

The child started sobbing.

"I want to see my mother first. I haven't seen her in three days, and I'm all scratched up from the branches."

It was on the tip of Marcus's tongue to tell the boy to leave at once and not see her, but if seeing his mother was what brought him back here, then that wouldn't be prudent.

He took a deep sigh and rolled his eyes at his generals.

"Very well. You may stay here one night with your mother, but then you must leave first thing tomorrow morning. You are dismissed."

The boy got up and ran out the door.

"Thank you!"

Marcus turned a pleased eye toward his generals as he updated the map with the scout's information.

"The chances of our success at taking out their southernmost defenses look better and better. It is as we suspected. They defend the coastline against our ships, but they are overconfident that we will stay here behind our wall and won't invade them on land, the way they raid against us. We'll slaughter these barbarians."

The Romans all smiled and laughed eagerly, discussing the details for a few hours — with one break to go out in the courtyard at noon and listen to the bagpiper.

A few hours before the slave girls would bring him his supper, Marcus signaled for his generals to leave his quarters and for his slave girls to give him another bath. He had just been dried off and dressed again in fresh clothes when the guard at his door ushered in one of the lower ranking members of the squadron he'd sent out yesterday to chase after the leader of the barbarians who inhabited the nearest rock hill, who had been found spying on them and defacing their wall.

This man also prostrated himself on the dirt floor.

Marcus signaled for two of the slave girls to give him a manicure and pedicure while he spoke to this man. It satisfied him to see them rushing about to get what they needed and hurrying up to get started.

He leaned back in his chair and watched them while speaking to the soldier.

"Report. And tell me why your captain isn't doing so, and why the report is so late. You should have been here last night."

The man drew in a ragged breath before he spoke, and when he did, he was sobbing almost as much as the boy had been. Well, not really. But he was sobbing.

Trying to cover it up, but sobbing nonetheless. It was impossible to get good help these days.

"Captain Terentius is wounded and being tended to, along with Rufus, Cato, and Tertius. It took the rest of us all night to carry them here, up and down the hills and through the thistles."

Marcus took a bit more interest in the report.

"Oh? Wounded how? And where?"

"Captain Terentius took sword wounds to his right arm and right leg—"

Losing his temper, Marcus stood up suddenly, throwing the two slave girls to the hard stone floor.

"I couldn't care less where on the captain's body the wound was, you dolt!" Marcus grabbed the soldier's hair and used it to hoist the man up where he could see the table. "Where on this map did the battle occur?"

The soldier studied the map with a surprising amount of intelligence in his eyes, considering how inept he had proven thus far. After a few moments, he calmly pointed to the forest about midway between Marcus's fort and the nearest rock hill.

"As you well know, the man is more slippery than quicksilver."

Grudgingly, Marcus nodded.

The soldier slowly shook his head no as he continued speaking.

"But this time we had him. He was all alone and cornered in a thicket here in this forest by the twelve of us. It should have been over. We should have brought you his head —"

Marcus shook the man a bit by his hair and yelled into his ear.

"Yes! You should have! By Jupiter, why didn't you?"

The soldier didn't resist, just put his hand out palm down and moved it parallel to the floor as he spoke calmly and again, with more intelligence than Marcus would've expected from a man his age — twenty or so.

"Out of the clear blue sky, a woman warrior joined him. By Athena, she must have fallen out of one of the trees of the forest and landed by his side, because at no time did we see anyone approaching him, and we had been following him closely ever since he left our wall. This woman picked up Captain's sword and ran to the barbarian's side, creating a bottleneck in the thicket such that none of us could approach the two of them without feeling the wrath of both of their swords. We tried, but after four of us had fallen, we admitted defeat and retreated. We fully expected the woman and the barbarian to kill the fallen, but they only looted them before they ran off. We came straight here and didn't see a soul on the way. And that's the end of my report."

Marcus got back into his chair and gestured his slave girls back over to resume work on his nails. He stroked his beard and looked at the familiar pattern of cracks in the stone wall.

"This woman warrior..."

"She was fierce, and oddly, she was dressed in one of our own tunics. Captain says she even had one of our helmets —"

Marcus cut the man off with a gesture.

"Yes I'm sure that's very interesting, but was she beautiful?"

The soldier cleared his throat.

"I'm sorry, did you ask if she was beautiful?"

Marcus felt his temper rising again. The urge to grab the man and by the throat and throttle him was almost overpowering, but he thought better of it. Because how would a throttled soldier answer any questions?

Marcus settled for pounding the arm of the chair with his fist.

"Yes, I did. Don't play the fool with me, soldier. I can tell you're a man of intelligence, so use it. Tell me what this strange fighting woman looked like, and spare me no details."

ELEVEN

S unlight was creeping in through the cracks on the other side of the tiny room at the top of the broch when Jaelle awoke. She wasn't confused at all about where she was, but she was ever so grateful that Kelsey had made her tour her memories, because she recalled very clearly where the nearest earthenware pot was, and she needed it desperately. She had slept in the plaid dress and the leather shoes, so she just got up and headed two flights down, listening to Breth and a bunch of other people talking on the fourth floor.

"Aye, messengers came in from brochs two through four while you were gone."

"what do they say?"

"There have been three more attacks in the last three days."

"Marcus appears to be making a last ditch attempt to get his precious wall built."

"He's attacking all up and down the construction..."

Jaelle was thankful that even though these people went about naked when they were ritually decorated for battle, they appreciated privacy when relieving themselves. A small straw booth had been constructed around the earthenware pot with soft green leaves left nearby for wiping, and there was even handmade soap and a pitcher of wash water.

The smell of food cooking on the fourth level drew her just as much as the voices, and she rushed up there, unsurprised to see Breth and Deoord and several other people sitting around the table waiting for their food while a couple cooked what smelled like eggs and some unfamiliar vegetables. Everyone was sandy haired and blue eyed like Breth.

He smiled at her and gestured to the empty seat beside him.

"Everyone, this is Jaelle, the one the future druids sent us. We must make her feel welcome."

Except for one woman who brooded, they all smiled at her and then waved or nodded as Breth named them. Jaelle knew there was no way she would remember everyone's name, but she tried.

"Jaelle, this is my father Eddarrnonn and my mother Almba, and my brother Talorac. And these two over here cooking are my father's brother Lutrin and his wife Fondla. This is my other uncle, Wroid, along with his wife Heulwen. You know Deoord, and these are our other three druids: Ia, Boann, and Nechtan."

Breth then turned toward the door, where three

people sat apart, dressed, but decorated in woad none-theless.

"Gest, Uvan, Dhori, go to brochs two, three, and four, respectively, and tell them what I've just told you about all I saw while I spied on Marcus the other night. Tell them the time is coming when we must raid again. Ask for a meeting in the sacred grove a fortnight hence. Go, run like the deer."

The three lean runners, two men and a woman, nodded and left immediately with nothing but the clothes and swords on their backs.

Wanting to ask what they were going to eat on their trip but afraid to hear the answer, Jaelle stood back to get out of their way and then went and sat next to Breth.

The brooding woman waved her hand in the air, and Breth turned to her as if she had just come in.

"Oh and this is Morna, the daughter of clan chief Ciniod."

Uh oh. Morna smiled at Breth when he introduced her, but whenever no one else was looking, she glowered at Jaelle with a look that unmistakably meant 'drop dead — or at least get out of here — because you aren't welcome.'

And of course Jaelle said the first thing that came to her mind — or rather her mouth did. Sometimes she was convinced it was trying to get her killed and thought it would live on without her.

"Hello Morna. Are you here as some sort of foreign exchange student, or are you a foster child here, or what?"

Yeah, and as it often happened when she didn't guard

her loose tongue, it had come up with the wrong thing to say.

If Morna's hidden scowl was hostile before, it was now outright murderous. But Morna was by far more skilled in the social graces, and Jaelle watched her in fascination, ready to learn. Morna leaned back and smiled at Breth's parents, uncles, and aunts, nodding slightly when they smiled back at her in a friendly way that apologized for Jaelle's presence, Morna soaked up their apologies and looked so grateful that they even started looking doubtful about accepting Jaelle, who was obviously upsetting Morna by sitting next to Breth at his invitation.

Wow, Morna was a grandmaster at social manipulation.

For a moment, Jaelle wished she had her phone so she could video this. And then she realized how difficult that would be to explain to these intelligent but non-technological people and was glad she didn't have it.

When Morna spoke at long last, her voice wasn't at all catty or snarky or unpleasant in any way. No, it was gracious and ladylike and above reproach.

Score fifty points for Morna.

"Yes, Jaelle, it's something like that. My father is the leader of another branch of our kingdom's people. He sent me over to stay with Eddarrnonn and Almba as a ... bit of a foster child, yes, you could put it that way. My mission is to spread goodwill between our clans. To get to know them and to perhaps think of them as family. Maybe even to join their family someday."

Jaelle couldn't resist looking at Breth to see what his opinion of this was. Did he like the idea? She looked over at him to see. Well, if she was being honest, mostly she wanted to see if he was ashamed for making it seem last night like he was available and single and unattached and everything he had said teasingly to her.

She couldn't believe it.

He was smiling at his younger brother and nudging him, convinced that Talorac was the target of this match-making on their parents' part. Could he really be that clueless? That ignorant of the looks Morna was giving him?

Apparently so.

When Breth caught Jaelle looking at him, he winked at her and rolled his eyes toward his brother as if to say, 'be glad you aren't part of a clan chief's family and don't have to go through all these machinations like poor Talorac over here. Isn't he pitiable?'

Fortunately, out loud Breth changed the subject, speaking with excitement.

"After we eat, we will all be going with the druids. It is our custom that I as the lead fighter of our clan and Father as the lead planner and the older members of our family help them prepare the sacred grove for a meeting. Will you come with us?"

Jaelle had heard about the druids' ceremonies, and before she could stop it, her mouth babbled about it.

"How do I know I'm not coming along as your human sacrifice?"

Everyone except Morna laughed, which put Jaelle a

little more at ease, seeing as how it wasn't a cruel laugh but one of mirth. Even Breth's aunt and uncle who were passing out plates of eggs and veggies joined in on the fun.

Breth picked up what looked like a slice of cooked eggplant, folded it in half, and used it to scoop up some eggs while he spoke to her through his laughter.

"Our people haven't performed human sacrifice in hundreds of years."

Resolving to just never look at Morna, Jaelle felt the bag that was tucked into her belt to make sure the helmet was still there and then folded her own slice of eggplant and dug into her eggs.

"All right, then. Yes, I'll go with you."

TWELVE

The walk to the sacred grove was like a party, save for the weapons everyone but the druids wore. The whole way there, the druids sang in a language that must have been even older than the Pictish one she was speaking with Breth. Many of the roots were the same, and she could catch some words of it, but most of it was just gibberish — especially because they were singing rather than talking.

"Breth, what are they singing about?"

He twinkled his eyes at her, wrinkling his nose.

"They sing of spring blossoms and fall leaves, of running deer and soaring egrets, the moon on the waters of the loch, and the wind whistling through winter's barren branches."

She gave him a tight sideways smile.

"If you don't want to tell me, just say so. I'm a big girl. I can take it."

This comment made him throw his head back and laugh so that his chest shook.

She enjoyed watching that.

He threw his arm around her and walked with her as if they'd known each other all their lives, weaving back and forth to the rhythm of the druid song.

"Oh, but I did tell you."

Her heart soared at the feel of him holding her.

But then the druid Nechtan popped up between them, and Breth laughed and let the man butt in, letting go of her.

Looking comically full of himself, the little man proceeded to lecture Jaelle.

"This is one of many ancient songs that have always been among us. It is our same language, just an older version of it, from when we used to change our words more than we do now. Songs preserve those things, you know."

Feeling a bit uneasy and not knowing why, Jaelle gave the druid her best 'Oh really?' nod — and then rushed back over to Breth's side, where she remained the rest of the way to the sacred grove, allowing Breth to translate the songs for her and looking about uneasily for the little druid man, who fortunately had been called up front by Breth's father, clan leader Eddarrnonn.

Morna scowled at her a few times, but other than that, the rest of the walk was pleasant.

When they arrived and the druids spread out, gesturing for the rest of them to sit down in a circle, the beauty of the sacred grove enchanted Jaelle, mostly because she was sure there were no tall thick old trees like this in Scotland in her day. The trees seemed to dance for her benefit in the wind, bringing back a distant memory of a family reunion years ago when she was a child in Washington State.

Her grandparents told her about a large local landmark the Indians had made reportedly as a burial site. The size of a twenty story skyscraper, it was called Grand Mound. She was excited to see it. But when they got to the spot where it should have been, Grandma and Grandpa couldn't find the mound. Distressed, they looked all over for this very popular monument that the town was named after.

Finally, one of the locals asked them what they were looking for, and on hearing it was the grand mound, gestured over and said, "Don't you see it? It's right there."

The three of them looked over and saw what looked like a mountain of trees.

Grandma gave Jaelle a worried look.

"Those trees weren't there when we were growing up here, your grandpa and I. The mound looks entirely different. The whole town looks entirely different than when we left here sixty years ago. It doesn't even feel like the same place."

Because of this painful experience with her grandparents, Jaelle knew that modern maps of forests would be useless to her during this time. If plant life could change that much in sixty years, how much more would have changed in two thousand years?

And then something happened that Jaelle should have been prepared for psychologically but was not.

Everyone stripped down and looked at her to do the same. Morna with a sneer.

When Jaelle froze there with her mouth hanging open, Breth looked at her with amusement in his eyes.

"I thought you understood that for ceremonies we go natural and have the druids decorate us with their ritual woad. It's a great honor for you to be invited along, which as the emissary of the future druids we owe you. Don't you want to participate?"

She turned crimson.

"I can see how you would think I understood that, but this is so foreign to me that I... It never crossed my mind that I would be..."

What should she do? She was dying to see what these rituals were like. The knowledge would be so useful at her job. She would have stories to enthrall the toughest crowds, even people like Fat Grandpa the next time she encountered one of those, which happened often.

Emboldened by the fact that everyone else had stripped and she wouldn't be alone in it, she did so, even putting the leather sack with the Roman helmet down on top of her pile of clothes. With her eyes on it in a bit of worry, she walked over to where the line of druids was decorating the line of laymen with woad grease they had brought along with them in earthenware jars.

Jaelle fell into the line between Breth and his mother. The grease was cold. The experience was anything but.

"But I know the woad decorations are needed

according to your traditions, and of course I will go along with that—"

She broke off what she was going to say, because Breth's eyes were mocking her playfully. He spoke in a teasing way, not as if he meant it.

"You'll go along with that? Look, if you don't want to be part of our traditions, then why don't you just go home, future woman?"

In fact his eyes were laughing so much that she forgot everyone else was there for a moment and just stared at Breth's glimmering blue eyes.

Deoord cleared his throat.

"Look, if you have... unfinished business to attend to, then I can come back later..."

Breth squeezed her around the waist. But then he looked toward the noon sky and sighed, then gently nudged her waist toward the druid.

"Tempting, but no. We really do need to get started."

Jaelle tried again.

"Why don't we just do the woad decorations tomorrow? There must be other things we could do today."

Breth and Deoord shared a look that said she really was a future woman and they had their hands full trying to make her understand their way of life. But the future druids demanded it of them.

Deoord decorated Breth's naked body just as complexly as it had been when she met Breth, but with different animals and creatures this time who were just as animated and fascinating and artful. Jaelle particularly liked the owl montage that now covered Breth's back. When he flexed, the owls took flight.

And as the druid made all these wonderful woad markings on that beautiful man's bare skin, he patiently explained.

"These markings are protective, not really decorative — although they are that as well. The drawings are infused with my magic, and my magic is the most strong when enacted here by these waters which feed our sacred grove..."

Deoord spoke all the while he decorated Breth's entire body, and when he was finished, he turned to Jaelle and gave a look that asked if he was to decorate her as well.

And she stood resolute and nodded yes at him.

It was almost unbearably weird to have a stranger she wasn't interested in touching her naked body, albeit to paint her with the woad.

But it helped immensely that everyone around her was participating in this ritual as well. And smiling about it.

The small magic man had finished decorating her left arm and was moving to her back when he paused.

"Do you have an affinity with any particular animal? Any that befriended you or that you tried to kill but couldn't, or that you tamed? Decorations made with such an animal will make my protective magic even stronger."

This gave Jaelle pause. She'd never had any pets. Her dad was allergic.

"No real animals, but I do love the idea of dragons. I don't suppose that helps, though."

But at this, she felt his hand going into furious motions on her back, spreading the blue grease in a wide span that she thought must be a wing.

His voice was as steady as ever while he worked, calming her.

"That's not just an idea. Dragons are every bit as real as horses or owls, and they are the patron animals of druids! Many think the various breeds of dragons went extinct in the age when the earth was covered in ice, but the dragons who went deep into the sea survived. Good on you. The dragon is a very strong patron animal. My magic will protect you well, so long as you wear this woad."

Jaelle couldn't see the flying dragon on her back, but Deoord put several serpent type dragons on her legs, coiling around them through the gaps in her muscles. His artwork was exquisite, and she could've easily sat there for hours, just watching the dragons seem to swim around her legs when she moved them.

Once each person was decorated, they sat down in the center of the sacred grove. Jaelle was the last to join them.

She turned to Breth.

"So what did Deoord mean when he said the woad was filled with protective magic?"

Instead of speaking, with one accord everyone got up and backed away so that they were standing in a large circle, leaving the center open.

Two naked blonde warriors got their weapons and moved into the center space.

The bout that resulted was just as tough as any Jaelle had fought against Cinnead, but these women were fighting naked — and with steel, not padded wood.

They were fighting hard.

And no blood was spilled.

Jaelle sat forward gawping at them with her jaw dropped open.

Breth took her gently by the arm, speaking to her softly.

"Are you glad now that you 'went along with our tradition' of the woad?"

Dumbstruck, all she could do was nod, making him chuckle. After a long while, she found her voice.

"It seems like you're invincible and should never lose a battle."

Breth spoke with his hand on her arm, holding it tenderly.

"No, we are far from invincible. For one thing, a druid's ritual woad magic only lasts two days, after which we have to give him at least that long to rest. —Oh, and this is important for you to know: while the woad protects the skin from being cut, it doesn't prevent blunt force from overcoming us. We are very careful not to let the enemy know this critical piece of information, however."

She looked up into his tender blue eyes, inches from her face.

"Good plan."

They searched each other's faces for a good long

while before Jaelle remembered they weren't alone and looked away from those blue eyes a moment.

And saw couples lying down together in the wet green grass.

Deoord lay with Boann, and the male druid named Nechtan moved toward Jaelle, while the female druid named Ia moved toward Breth, as did Morna.

But Breth stopped that in a hurry, shaking his head quickly at Ia and Morna and turning toward Nechtan in anger.

"Jaelle is very clearly with me."

Morna stared daggers at Jaelle and then skulked off.

Nechtan raised his chin at Breth and looked at Jaelle with interest.

"Not so clearly. You've only just met her."

THIRTEEN

Breth squared off on Nechtan, puffing his chest out and looking down on the smaller man.

"She is very much with me, and you will leave her alone."

Nechtan raised an eyebrow at Breth and dipped his chin with a mocking smile, all the while looking every bit the threat.

"Strong emotion for someone you've just met. Is there some history we should know about with the two of you?"

The druid then turned his back on Breth as if the warrior didn't worry him at all and commenced studying Jaelle's naked body even more intently, with even more interest.

It gave her the creeps.

But Breth took up his sword and swooshed it, moving in to settle the matter.

"You overstep your authority, Nechtan. And you will stop."

Jaelle found herself ten feet from the two men without even realizing she had backed away. Her eyes were glued to the drama, but her mind was whirling with what Breth had said.

Was she with Breth?

And for how long?

She really wanted to be with him, but how would that work?

She couldn't bring him home to her time. Try as she might, she couldn't make herself picture him in a car. Or wearing sneakers. Or opening a refrigerator. He was like a wild animal who just wouldn't be happy in a cage amid all the unnatural things, no matter how big that cage was. No matter how much love she gave him.

She could stay here, she supposed, and use the helmet to go home and visit. Even use it to go to the doctor if she needed to. And see her parents. And get her favorite snacks. And watch her favorite shows. Finding herself grinning inappropriately — given the showdown happening in front of her — she smoothed a hand over her mouth.

But then Nechtan raised up his hands menacingly toward Breth.

Jaelle gasped, knowing about druidic magic from John.

Yet Breth stood straight and tall, moving directly between her and the druid with focused slow deliberateness.

He reminded her of a cat stalking its prey.

And then things got weird.

The ivy Nechtan was standing near animated. Meaning it moved around like an animal. Quickly, it flung its ends up into the air and grabbed Nechtan's arms and legs, immobilizing him.

At the same time, Deoord called out from the other side of the clearing in the sacred grove.

"Nechtan, what's gotten into you? Go back to the broch and send Gede in your place."

The vines loosened and then slid down Nechtan's body and crawled back into their original places on the ground. Once there, they ceased being animated and were once more just vines of ivy.

Thanks to her trained fighter's reflexes, Jaelle noticed a noise off to her left and looked up just in time to see Nechtan lunging toward her.

She sidestepped him.

Concurrently, Breth stepped in, slashing Nechtan in the leg and speaking with cold harshness.

"Never mind. Jaelle and I will go back to the broch. You all stay here and prepare the grove for the meeting without us."

He took her gently by the arm and escorted her over to get their things. Finally, they left the area together, Breth looking over his shoulder the whole time. The look in his eyes dared Nechtan to follow them.

Her feet were tender. She hadn't gone barefoot since she was a child. Walking so through the forest was trying, but the feel of his hand on her elbow supporting her the whole way was thrilling. Something told her that if she fainted or tripped, he would pick her up and carry her. It was tempting, very tempting to fake a trip.

After they had walked a ways, he stopped her.

"You can put your shoes on now. And the rest of your things, if you like."

She had never been nude in the middle of a forest before, but it had seemed less odd while they were moving. Out of habit, she now looked around for a private place to change. And then laughed at how silly that was when she was already showing everything.

He laughed with her, an easy comfortable laugh.

What followed seemed like its own ritual.

To the accompaniment of birdsong and with the trees and the squirrels as their witnesses, they both dressed deliberately and with intensity, watching each other as they pulled their clothes on over the markings. Watching each other's muscles animate the illustrations was almost more sensual then actually touching would have been. He was so magnificent. Marked with the woad as he was, Breth looked perfectly natural against the grass and the flowers, the rocks and trees, and the distant cloudy Scottish sky.

His eyes were bluer than the woad, and each time hers wandered to them from the rest of his body, they pierced right into her again. They made her feel as if the two of them had already made love and this was the aftermath of it, his look was so intimate, so knowing. So aware of her and nothing else.

Eye sex.

In the briefest of fleeting thoughts, she realized this was what she wanted from a man: his absolute and undivided attention in moments like this.

This was what had lacked toward the end of her relationship with John. Oh, at first it had been like this, all starry eyed stares and delighted smiles. But they had let things creep in between them so that his duties took over his thoughts and then finally he found someone else who he was paying absolute attention to. He mistook that for better love than she could give.

But this was only a fleeting thought.

And she pushed it aside immediately, for these precious minutes were all Breth's and hers. She savored every second.

Even so, too soon those minutes had passed, and they were on their way down the road together once more, both clothed this time, and Breth apologizing for his clan's wayward druid.

"I'm sorry about back there."

She turned her head and gave him her most accepting smile, then quickly turned once again toward the faint trail back to the broch, amused that now she did not want to trip so he would carry her. She didn't want him to think her a fool.

"It wasn't your fault. You stopped him. Thank you."

He shook his head no and gave her a pained look.

"You misunderstand."

She held his look and gave him a puzzled one of her own.

"How?"

"I should have killed him for the way he was looking at you."

Wishing he had but knowing that was wrong, she turned away as if it were nothing and started walking toward the broch again.

"Oh no. He just got carried away."

He fell in beside her and took her hand as if they'd been walking together their whole lives.

"No. He was fully in control of himself and deserved to die — both for presuming about you and for gainsaying me. But we need him, my clan. We need his knowledge, and so I am sorry, but I could only wound him."

They were walking on in silence while Jaelle digested this when they first heard distant screaming and the clash of weapons.

Breth broke into a run.

"That's home — and I smell smoke."

Jaelle ran after him, and when she rounded the bend in the trail and cleared the trees, she clearly saw the broch under siege. A hundred Roman soldiers wearing mini-dresses surrounded what was now a pile of rocks with a burning thatched roof.

Breth's clan members inside were screaming.

A voice came from behind Jaelle and Breth.

"Shall we do one running attack before we retreat to number three?"

Jaelle turned and saw a man hanging upside down from a tree.

The woad falcon on Breth's face took flight when Breth smiled at the man in the tree, turned toward the broch, and drew his sword.

"Aye, that we shall."

FOURTEEN

Marcus marched in the rear of the regiment, shouting orders for his five ceremonially toga'd bagpipers to play whenever his soldiers broke the formation he had put them in so carefully.

"Hold the line!"

"Mind the corner!"

Why did men think just because there was a rock or tree in their way they had to break formation? They ought to hold a straight-line around such obstacles. Wasn't that why they drilled daily? You would think they sat around on their lazy backsides the way the savages did, his men were so incompetent at marching.

He would have to fix that when they returned to the fort. These men had only been marching half a day. They should be able to hold up this long and more. They were such an embarrassment to him that for once he was glad they weren't on the mainland, but rather on this Zeus-forsaken island.

He let out all his breath, burbling his jowls as he did.

One of his heralds looked at him in a less than respectful manner.

Marcus backhanded the little man.

Oh, who was he kidding?

He would yank out his eyeteeth if it meant he could return to the mainland and all the comforts there. Well, he would yank out a slave's eyeteeth. Rank has its privileges, so they say.

He exaggerated a sigh for the benefit of his generals around him before he raised his voice so that he could be heard by his bagpipers — since his herald was out of commission.

The bagpipers played the tune that signaled Marcus's command at the only volume bagpipes could play: loud enough so that everyone for miles could hear. But of course only Romans would understand.

"To the top of the far hill. Hold all spears level."

Marcus smiled with satisfaction.

This rocky and mountainous territory was marvelous for the use of bagpipes. Much better than anywhere he had battled on the mainland. How the noise echoed, announcing his arrival miles before he appeared. It couldn't get any better.

He gazed admiringly at his bagpipers. They merited their togas. Yes, they did.

And Mars must have blessed him at last, because his men were actually following orders for a change.

This way, the enemy would hear them coming and run into their rock hut. More of the enemy would die in the rock hut, seeing as how Marcus was going to use fire. But he hoped a few stayed out to fight. It would be so satisfying watching the barbarians die at the hands of his soldiers. And he had no doubt his confounded soldiers could take the enemy once they did reach them.

Because the foolish savages didn't wear armor.

Marcus was even happier when his men halted at the top of the far hill. He told his pipers to announce that they should attack whatever they saw on the other side — after surrounding them first.

He and his generals all held out their arms out and stood with their legs at parade rest so that their slaves could armor them up from the nearby wagons.

Marcus enjoyed this immensely, being able to armor only at the last moment in front of men who had been made to march in their armor. He was absolutely certain that every man there envied him the ability to walk about armorless. It was so much easier. He smiled smugly at his generals.

They returned his grin.

Once Marcus was encased in two finger breadths of leather, he gave the signal and his bagpipers changed their tune.

His men moved in for the kill.

Marcus was a tad bit disappointed. Most of the confounded breek-wearing enemy had escaped over the next hill with much of their livestock — instead of staying to fight. And some of the savages were trapped inside the burning hut screaming, so that he couldn't see their deaths.

But other than that, the battle was playing out satisfactorily, with gory bloodied deaths happening left and right in full view. The barbarians were odd even in death, wearing those strange breeks that separated their legs from each other. How did they urinate without exposing themselves? Of course, often as not they went about naked, so why would they care? How primitive.

And then that pesky enemy commander Breth and his exotic woman with the short curly dark hair led a charge down the far hill into the backs of his soldiers, who were pressing in toward the rock hut.

Marcus watched in fascination as the odd woman swung one of his own Roman swords. She must have picked it up from of the fallen men of the squadron he'd sent after Breth the other day, when he was spying on the fort from The Emperor's wall.

She used the sword skillfully, fighting off all attackers and not taking any hits herself. But she used an odd sort of rhythm that didn't quite match up with anything he had seen before. He wanted to see more. Up close and personal. Maybe have her give him lessons in that rhythm. Oh yes...

But as soon as Marcus got the idea to have the strange beauty captured, his least favorite enemy leader signaled a retreat. Breth and the buxom sword dancer were gone before Marcus could put words to his imagining and thus make it come to pass.

Oh well. The screaming inside the huge crude rock

structure had stopped, which meant it was time to go in and purge the place of all the remains of these vermin.

Again, Marcus told his commands to his bagpipers.

They changed their tune, spreading his word among the common men.

"Go inside that odd structure and burn everything that will burn. Be thorough."

There.

That would give Breth a reason to come attack Marcus's fort. The rhythmic woman obviously didn't leave Breth's side, so she would come along.

And Marcus would be ready for her. Yes.

Breth would bring her right into Marcus's trap.

FIFTEEN

Bloodied from battle but not bleeding himself, Breth looked around for Jaelle with equal parts excitement and anxiety. It would be fine if she had died. He hadn't gotten too attached to her yet. They didn't have any children, and he was still young. He would find another. Really, all would be right in his world.

His beating heart belayed the orders of his thoughts, however. She had better be hale.

Earth, please don't swallow her yet.

Leave her life energy inside her and allow her to yet breathe.

He concentrated on the life force he had sensed within her, willing it to still be strong and hearty. With his eyes closed, he sensed her life force coming near him, and he smiled, reaching out for her.

Her hand clasped his, and then she let go and patted

his back, misunderstanding the sorrow on his face, the earnestness of his wrinkled brow.

Hm.

So she had never been separated from a lover before during a battle. How was that possible?

Her voice was soft and low and honey sweet when she spoke near his ear, making him want to lean into her and let that voice run down his throat and into his stomach.

"I know many of your clan members died in the fire and in the battle. I'm so sorry for your loss. If you like, I can leave you alone for a while. I'll just go over and talk to the women—"

Quickly so she wouldn't escape, he opened his eyes and retook her hand, using it to pull her toward him into a quick embrace even as he looked her all over, making sure she wasn't wounded.

Whew.

She wasn't.

She didn't move away from his embrace. No, she yielded to it completely, looking up at him perfectly content and relaxed before he pulled away again.

He liked studying the depths of her brown eyes.

"The last thing I need right now is to be alone. I'm glad to see you're still breathing."

But far from having the expected effect on her, his comment made her laugh a bit through her nose, an odd laugh that was rather stifled, yet attractive in a way he hadn't seen before and didn't understand. He supposed that made her even more enticing. She was an enigma, and he enjoyed a challenge.

Her eyes turned into teasing pools of mirth, but they were still kind. Playful rather than wicked. He liked it.

"Well I'm glad you're still breathing, too."

A dozen or so other clan members were still out here, and they all came over to join him for the walk to their prearranged meeting spot for situations like this — which happened to be the sacred grove he and Jaelle had just left.

On the walk back, Breth took reports from everyone and got a good idea who had survived and who had died. The fighting force was largely intact. Most who had died were past the age of warriorhood or too young to have started.

Several turned to him for his revenge plan.

"When do we attack their fort, Breth?"

"Yeah, when will we get them back?"

Knowing they needed reassurance that he was in control of the situation even though he wasn't, he gave them his most confident look.

"We need to wait until after the meeting we called, in a fortnight. Or at least until the messengers come back and let us know if the other clans have accepted the meeting time."

And then Jaelle turned to look at him with a fire in her eyes that amazed him.

"I say we go right now."

He grinned and gave her another embrace, this one not so quick. This wasn't even her clan. Yet.

"Hold that thought — for we will go, once all the clans are gathered."

When they got to the sacred grove, they made camp with the supplies they had stowed there, for such a time as this. And once it was dark and the smoke wouldn't give away their position, they built a large bonfire in the clearing and took up positions all around it with their faces illuminated by the flames.

As the dead's clan members, it was their duty to stay awake all night in remembrance, telling each other their strongest memories of each person who had passed on to the next life.

"The day my father and I hunted the boar together is still my proudest moment as a hunter. It was my first kill of a large animal, and I am grateful that he let it be mine. He always was considerate, thinking of who might like to be the one dealing the killing blow this time. He was a fine hunter and could have taken them all himself..."

"My daughter had not yet taken her first steps, but she had a laugh that reminded me of the lovely goats braying. It brought our family much joy. May she have more luck in the next life than she had in this one, because she deserves it, being such a happy soul..."

"My husband always loved it when I sang this song. It would make him smile and look at me as though the world had been handed to him. And so I sing it now for him one last time, hoping that he smiles on his way into the next world..."

On into the night they talked, and the clouds gave way to the vast expanse of all the stars in the heavens, representing the souls of all who had gone before and yet still had not found their next world, shining down upon everyone in their benevolence.

"My brother was the best at carving the story pictures. I know he is happy that he has left them all behind as a permanence in this world that we can all remember him by. I will make a trip to the wall to see his masterpiece one last time before I leave this world, or I will leave this world trying to get there..."

At this one, Jaelle turned to the woman who had spoken — Gisa, who had lost her brother that day.

"You mean your brother's carvings are in the wall that the Roman Emperor Hadrian builds? Why would he carve there?"

Gisa turned to Breth and pleaded with her eyes that he would explain to his new friend and save her the trouble so that she could continue to maintain her wakefulness in her brother's honor without distraction.

Breth nodded to Gisa and then turned back to the one he wanted to make his.

JAELLE DRANK in the scene around her, it was so rich in the culture and history and lore that she and her friends wondered the most about: the ancient Scots. She had never imagined enjoying a wake, but then she had never been to one and hadn't known what she was missing.

The wake was like every other type of family gathering rolled into one — and nothing like a funeral. Oh sure, people were crying. But they were laughing too, sometimes at the same time. Rather than dwell on someone's death, they were celebrating each and every clan member's life that had ended today.

The women mended or embroidered as they talked and told stories and laughed and sang songs — all while remembering the departed who had grown up with them.

The young men and women went out on a hunt and came back with a deer, which they roasted over the bonfire on a spit and then carved out for everyone to eat, with leftovers for the morrow.

The older men whittled wood, or worked leather, or knapped arrowheads while they stood and laughed heartily and even shed tears for those who had passed beyond their knowledge — for now, as they said.

The children played extra exuberantly, running in and out of the trees in an elaborate game of tag that resembled those Jaelle herself had played as a child. The biggest tree was their safe spot.

It was fun to watch them. They didn't have toys so to speak, but they didn't lack for having fun. They ran about and laughed and chatted with each other, telling stories and making up fantasies.

In fact, Jaelle's favorite memories of being a child were of playing pretend, much like this.

The grown-ups weren't any less happy about being outside. In fact they were enjoying it much more than they had the broch. They happily went about gathering leaves to make soft places to sleep and they carried water up from the river with an ease and an exuberance she didn't imagine she could ever muster for such a menial task.

But then Jaelle realized something. The common denominator between the joy of the children and that of the adults was ... they had each other. They had an ease and appreciation for each other's company that was missing in the modern world. They were ecstatic that they got to socialize with each other in person.

These people weren't waiting for the time when they could go off and be on their own and get on the internet and chat with strangers. Sure, they were missing out on all the knowledge and easy research being online provided. But she thought they had much the advantage because they were indeed without smart phones.

AND THE FACT is you can't miss something you never knew was there, right?

These people didn't have family time just once a week. All of their time was family time.

And all the grown-ups passed jars of honey mead around, and jars of a biting whiskey that Jaelle could only take one swallow of before it started her coughing and spluttering, much to everyone's amusement.

Guilt swamped her, and she turned to Breth to get it off her chest.

"That poor girl lost her brother, and I have to ask her about his carvings. Please tell her I'm sorry later, once she's over my rudeness."

But Breth turned to Jaelle and gave her a sympathetic friendly smile.

"Don't worry about what you said to Gisa. She understands your curiosity, and she is grateful that you take interest in her brother."

He looked over toward Gisa for confirmation of this, and Gisa smiled nicely at Jaelle before she went back to telling everyone else all the good things and funny things and otherwise remarkable things she could remember about a brother she must have loved very much.

Breth turned back to Jaelle on the log where he sat next to her and held out his arm.

Like a moth to a flame, she scooted up next to him and cozied into his warmth as he put his arm around her and held her with surprising tenderness and affection for a man of his warrior status. The incongruity of it made him even more attractive, as did the pleasing firmness of all his muscles pressing against her — almost like the hot rocks of one of those rock massages.

Making her shudder with the intimacy of it and waking up areas of her body that had been dormant six months, he leaned his head close to her and spoke in a rumbling deep voice very softly, so that his breath warmed the side of her face and tickled the inside of her ear.

"I told you about this already, but I saw how besotted you were with my naked body, so maybe you are too distracted to hear me. This time I hope you will listen better."

Making it as difficult for her to listen as possible, he

traced the very tip of his finger over the curve of her neck, right where it was the most sensitive, from just under her ear and down to her collarbone, still rumbling just above a whisper in his deep manly voice.

"I explained that we carve our stories into the rock where the story took place because this is where the story makes the most sense. And all of our stories these days are about our raids on the barbarians. We cannot let them finish their wall."

And then the two of them curled up together for warmth while they listened to everyone speaking and laughing and crying and singing. Some, particularly the children, were nodding and falling off their logs. Others were plain old passed out and snoring or showing other signs that they were having a difficult time maintaining their wakefulness.

Jaelle wasn't having that problem at all.

SIXTEEN

After the sun had been up for a while and they'd all eaten some porridge prepared over the bonfire just before it got light, the clan arranged watches so that they could sleep. Breth took first watch, and Jaelle slipped into a welcome oblivion.

She must've been sleeping quite a while before Amber and Kelsey stepped into her dream, because she wasn't feeling weary at all anymore.

Amber was looking at her with a combination of admiration and worry, mixed in with a little — horror? Oh yeah.

"That's quite a lot of battle blood you have all over you. I bet I wish I could see the other guy."

Jaelle hadn't consciously dreamed of wearing the blood marks on what was now her only set of borrowed clothes. She must have subconsciously been aware of them, because they still decorated her, even in sleep.

"Sorry, but I haven't had a chance to wash, and I

don't know where I would even if I did have a chance. Here, let me bring you up-to-date on what my day was like yesterday."

Morna's murderous scowl, the incident with Nechtan here at the grove, the walk back to the broch, and then the battle defending the broch from the Romans all played out in stunning detail, clear through the burning of the broch, the march back here to the sacred grove, and the wake.

Amber hugged Jaelle.

"Are you ready to come home yet?"

But Kelsey chuckled.

"Oh there's more, though."

She looked to Jaelle for permission of some sort.

When Jaelle shrugged, Kelsey played out last night's cuddle with Breth in fast forward, but it showed a lot of detail nonetheless.

Jaelle gave Kelsey a stare, trying to shame her for looking in on her private moments.

But Kelsey had asked permission. She just gave Jaelle a sweet look and turned to Amber.

"So you see, she probably wants to stay at least a little while longer."

Amber grinned at Jaelle with all of her teeth.

"You're falling for the Celtic man."

Embarrassed, Jaelle put on her haughty tour guide persona as a cover up.

"More specifically, he's a Pictish man, but even that's not what he calls himself."

Kelsey's interest must have been piqued, because she

strode on over to Jaelle and materialized some comfy dream chairs amid the sleeping bodies in the sacred grove.

The three of them sat down in a circle with Kelsey leaning forward on her elbows and looking up into Jaelle's eyes.

"Well, what does he call himself? Do tell. And you wouldn't believe how grateful I am that you let me hear the Pictish language during your memories of your day. Wow, huh?"

But at that reminder of all Breth had lost, sorrow came back to Jaelle.

She snubbed Kelsey minorly, for not answering her question — which her friend deserved for embarrassing her even if Jaelle had given permission — and turned to Amber.

"So did you find anything out about the battles that were fought at the wall close to the broch the Romans burned today?"

Amber gave her a sorry look.

"I searched the Internet for quite a while yesterday, but I couldn't find anything useful. I would probably have to go to one of the University libraries here in Scotland — or Kelsey could go to the one at Celtic University — and search through microfiche of actual documents."

Jaelle patted her friend's shoulder.

"I understand. And I hope you understand this is very urgently needed information, so I hope you will do so as soon as you can and then get back to me with it."

She looked back-and-forth between her two old

friends, searching their eyes and being mostly reassured by what she saw there.

"You will, right?"

Amber took her hand and gave her a look of promise and sincerity.

"For you, I will. I'll take a few days more here in Scotland before I head over to Australia. Tomas will understand. So will Dall and Emily."

Jaelle turned to Kelsey and gave her a look she hoped would shame her for being such a voyeur — and make her help.

Her friend looked worried, but determined.

"Yes, I will do this for you. We'll help you help your Pict man."

SEVENTEEN

Marcus drove his men hard, making them stay together in formation as they trained with sword and spear. They had to function as a unit, or they weren't doing it right. This was the way of the Roman army, and he would not have his men be an embarrassment on the off, off, off chance that anyone from the continent came to inspect them.

As a side benefit, it wouldn't hurt to have the men in top form when — not if — Breth came to avenge those who had been killed at his rock hut.

JAELLE AWOKE to a completely different sacred grove than she had fallen asleep in. It was now more like a home. A roof had been built over part of the forest, and it looked like it would protect them from the rain while sleeping here over the next several nights. The people had brought all sorts of things out of a small storage cave nearby. Bags of grain — perhaps barley — now accompanied the bag of oatmeal they had made a breakfast of this morning. Children were hauling blankets and cookware into the nearby shelter, along with pretty much everything else the clan needed to live there.

Breth's mother came up behind Jaelle where she lay in the clearing by the coals of last night's wake bonfire and put a gentle hand on her shoulder.

"I don't want to presume, but I imagine you would like to wash up."

Hope sprang into Jaelle's heart, and she let the kindly elder woman see it on her face.

"You must be reading my mind. There's nothing I want more right now than a bath — please remind me of your name?"

"Almba."

"Well lead on, Almba, and I hope you aren't teasing me. I hope I really can wash off all this blood."

Smiling in a knowing but kindly way, Almba led Jaelle through the forest for a bit. They passed children tending goats and chickens as they walked.

Jaelle kept looking back at the impromptu home that had been made there.

"How long will the clan stay here?"

Almba paused between the trees and leaned her head to the side for a moment, twinkling sky blue eyes that reminded Jaelle of her son's.

"Perhaps a moon cycle, perhaps less."

Jaelle turned her head slightly to the side and leaned

it forward a bit as the two of them resumed their walk along a faint path among the fallen leaves in the woods.

"And I thought my people moved around a lot. How can you be so satisfied with all this moving around? Don't you want a steady place to live, where you can put in roots? I was under the false impression that people from this time moved around far less than we do in the twenty-first century."

Almba waved her hand in the air briefly, taking in the trees and the mountains and even the cloudy Scottish sky.

"Oh no. Moving is part of life's natural rhythm. Only the dead stay still. We seldom stay in one place for more than two moon cycles at a time, though we do come back to the same places during the same times of the year each cycle."

So the Picts were nomads. Interesting.

Soon, they turned down a pathway that eventually led them to a large sandy shallow pool in the river. Many of the women were down there bathing — laughing and splashing and having a grand old time. They bathed in their clothes, which then were getting washed as well.

There was even soap.

A line of men stood guard around the perimeter, looking outward.

Almba saw Jaelle looking at them.

"They will sound an alarm at the first sight of any stranger, so go ahead. Take your ease. Bathe, and make yourself more comfortable."

Jaelle looked down at her feet doubtfully.

"Should I take my shoes off?"

Almba shook her head, wrinkling her forehead the slightest.

"No, the water will help shape them to your feet. Surely you know that?"

Jaelle laughed and waded in.

The cool water felt wonderful on all her sore muscles. Much sooner than she thought possible for her, she was submerged up to her neck. And sighing in pleasure. She turned to the older woman, who had followed her in and was nearby, making it easy for them to keep the conversation just between the two of them.

For some reason, Jaelle felt shy around talking about the future in front of everyone else. She knew they knew, but still. At least two of them had a bone to pick with her.

She chuckled a bit.

"The truth is, we know very little about such things in my time. Whenever something is wearing out, we just toss it and get something new. We don't make any of the things ourselves, either. We have no idea how to do it. I only own one pair of leather shoes. The rest are all made from what we call man-made materials—"

Seeing the overwhelmed and puzzled look on the other woman's face, Jaelle paused for a moment and really thought about what she was going to say.

For once.

"The short of it is, I live in a different world. Everyone is specialized in what they do, and each of us only knows how to do that one specialized thing. I give tours of a collection of things from this time. My older sister teaches young children how to read our picture drawings. My dad assembles one part of a rod we use to catch fish in our time. There are benefits to this specialization. We have much more complicated tools and clothing and shoes and houses and methods of transportation, communication, and even of applying medicine. But in exchange, I'm pretty much helpless here in your time. I don't even know how to make a dress, much less wear-in a pair of shoes. Those were things my grandparents talked about, but silly me, I never listened."

Almba gave Jaelle an amused look at this last bit.

"Well that hasn't changed in all the years between now and your time. No one listens to their grandparents now, either."

Jaelle giggled at this, and the two of them shared a companionable laugh.

And then out of the clear blue sky, Jaelle's mouth popped off again, saying exactly what was on her mind, much to her embarrassment.

"Is it all arranged? Will she have him no matter what?"

As soon as she heard her mouth say it, she wanted to suck the words back in — more than any she had ever said.

But Almba took Jaelle's hand and smiled a sad smile as she led her out of the water and over to a large rock, where they wrung out their dresses as best they could while still wearing them and then took clean seats to let the sun dry them the rest of the way.

"I suppose you've gone out of your way not to notice

what Morna was doing, and I can't say I blame you. She's left, Jaelle. She's gone back to see what she can find of her people. This broch wasn't the only one attacked, and she fears the worst."

Jaelle looked Almba in the eye for a somber moment.

"Such a tragedy."

Almba nodded, but then showed Jaelle the tiniest smile.

"Yes it is. But life goes on."

Jaelle gave Breth's mother her tiniest smile in return.

"Yes, that it does."

They didn't engage in any more deep conversation, but rather watched everyone playing in the water around them.

Jaelle felt that something had changed between her and Breth's mother, though. In a good way. She returned to the sacred grove refreshed and much better-looking, in her own opinion, not to mention better smelling. She was relieved to see and smell that the men and children had bathed as well, likely while she slept.

Breth's eyes lit up when he saw her coming, and he got up from his place amid the other fighters and saun- tered up to Jaelle with his chest all puffed out. He smelled like soap, thank the Lord.

"I see you found the bathing pools."

She gave him an amused smile.

"More likely, you —smell— I found the bathing pools."

There it was again, that amused smile that made his whole face light up and become ten times more handsome even than it was during repose. It wasn't right, for a man to be that handsome. But it felt wonderful to have him giving her that smile.

He gently took her hand and tugged her toward the new shelter.

"Come on, there's cold roast venison for lunch."

The food was still laid out on the trays, but it had been covered by many layers of linen. Instead of plates, they used large leaves from a nearby tree. In addition to the venison there was leftover porridge. It tasted okay cold with the meat.

Most of the other people had already eaten, but a few sat with them, smiling and chewing.

Once they were finished, Breth once again turned his intense gaze on Jaelle.

"You held your own pretty well during the battle. Will you take part in our training for the attack on the fort? I know you said you were ready to go attack the invaders right away, but we like to make sure we're in top shape, and we just spent twelve hours not fighting."

Everyone nearby laughed at this, a hearty laugh that came from the bottoms of their lungs and pushed out a great deal of noise. Even the women laughed this way, unlike the feminine giggle Jaelle's father had encouraged.

She looked around at all the faces. They were friendly. There was not an ounce of reproach or teasing or arrogance or any of the negative looks she would expect people to show an outsider when they are preparing for a battle after they had lost loved ones in their home.

Tears came to her eyes, she was so touched at their acceptance of her.

She looked around for Nechtan's leering face, but she didn't see it. Her gut told her to ask Breth where the druid was, but she didn't want to ruin this nice moment when everyone was making her feel so welcome. Maybe he had gone off somewhere too, just like Morna, and she could enjoy Breth's company in peace.

But she also didn't want Breth to get too big for his britches — now that he was wearing them. Feminine intuition told her that in order to keep this man's interest, she had to keep him on his toes. Keep him guessing at where he stood with her.

And so she put on some chutzpah, placing her hand on her hip.

"I figure I can take anything you guys can dish out. Lay it on me. Let's have some training, by golly."

She must've said the right thing, because everyone cheered.

Breth gave her a big smile and then stood and shouted out a bunch of directions which amounted to the non-fighters and children setting a watch and then all the fighters pairing off against each other in various small clearings in the grove for individual combat with the sword.

Jaelle found herself in single combat with Breth.

It wasn't a good test of her field abilities, of course. This was a duel, a 'one, two, three, go!' kind of thing. Out in the field you seldom got a warning when someone was about to attack.

This was more like a game, and she enjoyed it.

The two of them fought ten practice bouts. Breth won the first one. Jaelle the second. Breth the third, and so on. Jaelle won every other time.

They were both sweaty now, and they sat down in the wild heather among the trees, to rest and drink the water some children brought them.

After she downed most of her water, Jaelle gave Breth an 'I'm onto you' smile out of the side of her mouth while wrinkling her brow at him. And then she waited to see if he wanted to know what she was thinking. She was thankful that she didn't have to wait long, that he was genuinely interested in her thoughts.

"What makes you smirk so?"

She downed the rest of her water and handed the empty gourd to a passing child, who handed her a full one, which she also half emptied.

"You shouldn't have gone easy on me. I don't get the training I need unless I have to try my hardest, and I wouldn't have been upset if you had won every time. I expected you to, being much stronger than me and all."

He drank down his second gourd of water and chuckled.

"That cuts right to the heart."

She dipped her chin quickly.

"What does?"

He shook his head, giving her a wide grin.

"The fact that you beat me five times and you weren't even trying your hardest."

"Oh come on. You weren't trying your hardest either."

He leaned in closer, until his face was only a foot away.

"I was trying as hard as I could and not hurt you."

She scoffed.

But he cut her off, gazing into her eyes with admiration.

"You're an amazing warrior, Jaelle. Each time I figured you out, you changed the way you moved. Used new tactics. And most of your moves, I've never seen before."

Hm, maybe he was telling the truth. She did have the benefit of two thousand years of progress in sword fighting techniques, let alone SCA sparring partners from all over the world.

But she wanted to keep the mood light.

And keep him on his toes.

"Well I've never seen your moves before, either."

She playfully shoved him by the shoulder.

But this backfired.

Because his fighting reflexes were at least as fast as hers.

Gently but firmly, he grabbed her wrist and used her momentum to lie her down, pinning her the way a wrestler would, with her wrist on the ground and him leaning over her.

His eyes asked her a question as old as the mountains that surrounded them.

She wanted to be coy, but she knew she'd better give him a definite answer. Feminine intuition again.

"I want you Breth, but not like this. Not without a promise of faithfulness. And it's too soon to ask that of you. We've only just met. Let's give it some time, agreed?"

He slowly backed off, lifting her up so she was seated again on the flowers and greenery between the trees of the forest.

"Do we have time? Do you know when you'll be going back, or if? Deoord made it sound like the fae could take you at any moment. I thought we just had to enjoy the time we've been given. I would love to have more time with you. Much more. All your time..."

She was tempted to take this as a throwaway compliment, but he was sincere. It showed in the yearning gaze of his blue eyes and the set of his jaw, and she could feel it in the caress of his hand in hers. He was offering just what she wanted, and she needed to be honest with him. And forthright.

Gazing into the depths of those blue, blue eyes, she spilled her most vital secret.

"Deoord was protecting me when he implied that only the fae knew how long I would be here." She tapped the helmet in its bag. "I have the means to leave at any time. But I keep wanting to stay. And anyway, I've never used this before, so I don't know for sure, but I think I can probably leave and come back as many times as I want, so long as I have this. As for whether I'll stay here with you most of the time? Like I said, it's too soon for me to make that decision. I would need to spend at least half a year with you, before I would make that kind of commitment."

The wheels turned behind those blue eyes as he mulled this over, absorbing all that she had said. While he did so, a warm and joyful smile slowly but surely took over his whole face.

Before long, they were beaming at each other.

Not long after that, he once again had a question in his eyes. This time, it wasn't such a big question.

This time, her answer was yes.

Their kiss was electrifying, it was so full of chemical attraction. But he was also tender, even as his kiss promised her passion in their time to come.

"Dinner! Everyone come to dinner!"

Once they heard this, they smelled the delicious venison stew and helped each other up and walked over to the shelter arm in arm, to cat calls and whistles and smiles from all who gathered there for the joyous group meal that was a celebration of their clan's unity.

Over the next week, Jaelle trained with each and every fighter in the clan, teaching them all different moves. But she gave most of her time to Breth.

MARCUS SIGHED an extra heavy exaggerated sigh for the benefit of his generals, who were sitting on top of the stand with him in their comfy chairs, watching the men drill with spear and sword the way they had been doing for a week straight. The way Roman soldiers had been doing all his life.

He turned to the general on his right, a man he thought of only as his first general. In fact that was the man's rank, and that was what he called him.

"First General, do you think the men have done this drill enough times today?"

The man made a show of thinking it over, but Marcus knew he was just going to agree with him, and he appreciated that about the man. He had sense enough to defer to his better.

Sure enough, First General nodded at Marcus.

"Yes. After all, they do still need to eat before they sleep."

Marcus turned toward second third and fourth generals.

"Do you concur?"

Of course they all nodded yes.

"Yes."

"I do."

"As you say."

Marcus turned to his bagpipers and gave the orders which would put the men in their barracks for the night, where they would each be handed a bag of field rations consisting of hard jerky and prunes.

EIGHTEEN

J aelle woke up early in the morning. She was
cold, and she soon discovered the cause. Breth
had gotten up. He was missing from where they
had snuggled together every night under the
shelter out of the rain with everyone else.

In fact, all the fighters had gotten up.

Her feelings were torn between feeling left out and
being glad that they let her sleep. This week had been
thrilling, but exhaustingly physical. She had lost ten
pounds and looked almost as svelte as the other women.
Amber and Kelsey had teased her about it of course, to
the extent that she almost had to beg Amber to call the
museum and explain that Jaelle had left on an unex-
pected vacation and would be out a while. Both of her
friends had done the research she requested, but had
found nothing specific enough to help.

After running her hands through her hair and rinsing
out her morning breath with a mouthful of whiskey —

which served really well as mouthwash even though she couldn't drink more than a swallow without choking — Jaelle went in search of the fighters and found them by the river bank, thanks to directions from some of the children who ran back and forth everywhere, like lizards.

As she got close, she heard the fighters talking heatedly and rushed to see what was going on.

"Just the fact that they've attacked brochs two, three, and four as well means that we need to retaliate now, before they come back and finish us off."

"No, we need to wait for their runners to come back from brochs five, six, and seven. Help will come, just not as soon as we thought. We have enough supplies for another month here, at least—"

"What makes you think brochs five, six, and seven haven't been attacked as well?"

"She's right. The time for waiting on word from those who man the distant brochs has passed."

"I agree. It's time for us to take action. The invaders will expect us to wait for reinforcements. If we attack right now, we will have the element of surprise in our favor."

When Jaelle got to the group, she saw that the runners who had been sent out as messengers had returned. Gest, Uvan, and Dhori all smiled at her, and she returned their greetings.

Breth met her eyes and gave her a welcoming smile, too. He was downright stunning in his role as leader of the fighters, wearing command the way some men wear fashionable clothes.

"Jaelle, you get your wish," he said. "Tomorrow, we launch a surprise night attack on the fort."

He held out his arm to her, and she walked into it, where he held her by his side as he explained his plan to everyone gathered there.

An inexperienced woman might have thought his hold was casual, but Jaelle knew better. Holding her like this was Breth's way of declaring her his, and she knew just the man who this declaration was meant for. Her eyes automatically scanned the crowd for Nechtan, whom she hadn't seen much in the past week.

When she found the druid, he was looking the other way, rather on purpose, the way it seemed to her. Good. Hopefully there wouldn't be any more trouble. Jaelle had been called a drama queen before, but she was far from it. She disliked confrontation, actually. It was just that she wasn't willing to put up with people's BS. She always stood up for herself, but she never started the drama.

Grateful to have one less thing to worry about, she let her eyes wander back where they wanted to be.

Exuding confidence in his role as the leader of raids, Breth was showing the fighters the model he had built of the Roman fort and the nearby wall out of the wet sand on the riverbank. Using sticks and rocks and leaves, he showed them what they needed to do in order to make his plan for their surprise night attack work.

"Lutrin's group will cut off this gateway in the wall so that the twelve guards on night watch can't return to their fort. Talorac's group will take out those guards. Meanwhile, my group will sneak in over the wall on the other side. Any questions or advice?"

The fighters didn't raise their hands, nor did Breth call out names or use any signal that Jaelle recognized, but even so, only one person spoke at a time. It was a puzzle she worried in her mind throughout the whole conversation.

"You shouldn't sneak over the wall. It will take too long. Just go in through the gateway that the others will make clear."

Breth acknowledged the woman who had spoken with a polite nod and then shook his head no.

"They'll be expecting us to do that. When I say this is a surprise attack, I mean we're going to do what is least expected. Surprise is our only advantage, so we need to make the most of it. Climbing over the wall will allow us to take most of them in their sleep, and we will need to do that, seeing as how they outnumber us three to one. But I appreciate the advice. Keep it coming."

From her place of honor at Breth's side with his arm around her, Jaelle looked closely for some sort of signal to pass between Breth and the next person who spoke, but she saw none. Nevertheless, one man spoke up and everyone else remained quiet. She resolved to notice what the signal was the next time.

"Well then, if we're going to do what is least expected, then why have groups at all? Groups are expected and more easily seen and heard. Why don't we just go in pairs?"

Again Breth gave a polite nod, but this time he didn't

shake his head no. Instead, he began adding more sticks and more leaves and more stones to his model, spreading them out all around the outer edges of the fort.

"Excellent point. I agree. Groups are noisier and more conspicuous, and pairs will make it easier for us to surround them and come in from all directions. Yes, I like it. Let's go in pairs."

This started much talk and gesturing as everyone chose partners for the raid. Breth squeezed Jaelle's side, and she looked up at him to see a question in his eyes again. She nodded yes in answer, agreeing that they would be a pair, of course.

Once the side conversations had died down, again there was one single speaker, another man. And even as close as she was to Breth, she hadn't seen the man give any sort of signal to let breath know he wanted to speak. Her curiosity was just about killing her, but she resolved not to ask Breth about it. She wanted to figure this out on her own.

This man jumped up on top of a tree stump to be seen above everyone else and spread his hands wide with exuberance.

"To make it even more of a surprise, why don't we start on our way there tonight?"

At this, there was a general cheer, and all Breth had to do was nod.

Jaelle got caught up in the excitement. Okay, and the feeling of his arm holding her tight.

NINETEEN

Marcus slammed his fist down on the arm of his great chair, which he thought of as his throne.

"Yes, I said half the men will be on guard at all times, and that's what I meant. All the men need to do is guard and eat and piss and sleep. There is plenty of time to do all that with half of them on guard at any given moment. I'm not doing this for no reason. Breth's clan will attack us. It's a fact. We know for sure they're coming. We just don't know when, so we must be ready at all times."

First General put his fist to his heart and bowed his head.

"I hear and obey, Great Marcus. Will you permit a question?"

Marcus petted First General's hair as if the man were a loyal dog — and this was pretty much the way he thought of the man.

"Very well. What is your question?"

First general allowed himself to look up at Marcus's eyes with intelligence and amused awareness.

"Are you quite sure you won't know when the attack is coming?"

TWENTY

Breth and Jaelle spent the heat of the day in the river, alone in a secluded cove, just the two of them. They bathed well, and then Deoord came with his pot of blue goose grease and patiently waited on the riverbank.

This time, Jaelle was eager to be protected by the woad.

And then it was time to strap on their weapons — and her the helmet bag — and go.

Breth took her hand and guided her up the path to the makeshift shelter, where all the fighters waited nearby. They were similarly armed and decorated, and again it was tempting to stand and stare at the wonderful animated animals and plants that covered these naked people.

But perhaps aware of her difficulty in not staring, Breth took her by the arm and walked out in front of all the fighters, calling out behind them.

"The sooner we get started, the sooner we get our vengeance."

There was a general cheer that sounded more like 'rawr', and then the large party was on its way, wearing nothing but woad, shoes or boots, and hip or back scabbards with weapons.

For the first five hours, Jaelle assumed they would hunt for their supper. But subtly and gradually, it dawned on her that she wasn't getting hungry. Nor tired. Matter of fact, her muscles weren't getting cramped, nor her lungs stinging from the unusual amount of exercise, either, the way they had on the first leg of this round-trip.

She did get thirsty, as did everyone else, and every time they came to a source of water, everyone went down to drink, careful not to remove any of the woaded grease that decorated them.

The woad — or rather the druid magic infused in it — was obviously keeping the fighters in a state that at least didn't need food or rest, if not a state that replicated food and rest.

Wow.

The druids practiced very powerful magic, indeed.

The fighters walked all night, and then when the sun was coming up, Breth changed direction. Drastically.

Jaelle was dying to ask what the heck they were doing climbing up this craggy mountain when they were supposed to be going to the Fort to kick some butt, but her gut told her not to.

And for once, her mouth listened. Maybe the woad

gave her some sort of magical power over her mouth. That would be nice.

Instead of asking why — instead of talking at all — she observed the attitude of the people as they climbed the mountain. They were solemn and quiet. Reverent, but still not the least bit sleepy. Whenever her eyes met someone else's, they looked at her in calm serenity, sure they were on the right path.

She let that be enough.

But she soon learned that she didn't have to. The clan fighters' reward for the climb halfway up the mountain was a hidden sanctuary in the cleft of some boulders.

From a distance, it looked like a small animal cave. But when they got closer and went around the huge round rocks, the path went down into a cave that was big enough for all forty nine naked woad warriors to fit easily, sitting or lying down at their leisure. Even better, the cave floor had been covered with fresh rushes not terribly long ago. They were long past their fragrant green state but surprisingly soft and warm against the skin. Much less irritating than the straw bales Jaelle had sat upon long ago at the faire.

But the best part of the cave was that its walls were covered in Celtic carvings of the Pictish variety.

Jaelle sat down next to Breth and stared at all the carvings in the dim sunlight that penetrated into the cave.

"What does it all say?"

With everyone else listening and sometimes putting in a detail here or giving a demonstration there, the leader of the clan fighters spent a few hours telling Jaelle all the stories that were pictured on the dome cave wall.

It started on one side of the cave with the story of how long ago, the Picts had come over the large water from the mainland to live on this island, which they found enchanting and well suited for the Pictish way of life. Mountains for hunting the great birds. Grassy valleys for stalking the great stag. Great lochs full of seafood. This was paradise.

The people were depicted carving out their small boats and then rowing over the channel in them. Only three or four people fit in each boat, usually the parents with their small children. There were pictures of older children carving out and rowing their own boats.

Another sequence showed what the Picts had brought along with them from the mainland: their swords, of course, along with all the iron tools needed to make looms for weaving the linen for their breeks and dresses, arrows for hunting the great bird and stag, axe heads for chopping wood for the planks to floor the grand fortresses they would build...

Left behind on the mainland were many loved ones depicted, related clans who didn't want to come along. They were shown among their fine homes, flocks, and fields, saying 'What place could be better than home?'

Those who did come over here to found Pictland were shown as the adventurous ones. Hunters with weapons, rather than gatherers with baskets.

There were others shown to be here on the island when the Picts arrived, but so few of them and so few

Picts that they largely left each other alone. They were shown with their backs to one another.

But then new invaders came from every which way to try and take this land from the Picts. Angles, Saxons, Gaels, these new invaders from faraway Rome.

The Gaels were almost tolerable. At least the Gaels respected the clan structure. At least the Gaels only tried to take land for themselves, and only what they could use.

These invaders from Rome, howsoever, were a big concern. They weren't individuals. No, they were a collective. They acted on the mind of someone far away, and acted blindly, following without question orders which were against their own interests. That kind of thinking was dangerous. It needed to be fought.

In keeping with the celebration of individualism, the stories of many individual people were also depicted on the cave wall.

One especially pictorial story was about an early clan chief who had united what was then a record of three clans. He had done it to fortify a hill against all the other clans. The large man, nearly seven feet tall, was pictured with each of four wives, three of them dead, and then his seventeen children — fourteen of them sons. It was easy to see why he was so powerful.

Loyalty to parents was quite strong in this culture, which extended loyalty to a related clan chief. A clan was a family, and non-relative members were rare except in the case of marriage – and then of course, the person was joining a family.

All of the carvings in the cave made Jaelle gape in

wonder and awe. What a long record of the history of the people in such a simple way.

It made sense.

All the fighters came here year after year, sometimes bringing their children just to see the stories. They didn't need to turn the pages of a book in order to tell the story. The children could lie comfortably on their backs and gaze up at the pictures, learning how to discern what they meant as the parents told the stories.

Jaelle could imagine it all happening around her as they sat, the woad painted warriors, telling the stories as if they were her parents. It was a beautiful tradition, and she felt so honored to be included.

All the stories revolved around this very cave. In fact, while Breth spoke, his brother Talorc was busy carving in one small undecorated location, of which there were only a few.

After a time though, the stories had all been told, and the group's whispered discussion turned toward reiterating their plan and wishing each other a good battle.

Throughout this whole span of six hours or more, none of them got hungry, they passed skins of water around — and only one person was speaking at a time.

But once again, there was no visible signal they were giving, nor any visible signal from Breth to the person whose turn it was to speak. Baffling.

Jaelle had a question for Breth, but she didn't want to interrupt this odd conversation. So she turned and looked him in the face and waited for his eyes to meet hers.

This took a while, because he was looking at the

person who was currently speaking, and then he looked at someone else and they spoke...

Oh!

How simple. She felt like an idiot for not catching on before, and she slouched where she sat, deflated. But she kept looking right at him.

Sure enough, when Breth at last turned to Jaelle and met her eye, she just knew that was the signal and it was her turn to speak. She took a deep breath in order to bolster herself up enough to speak confidently, and then addressed everyone.

"I am honored to be along with you on this quest for vengeance. Thank you for your faith and trust in me. From the way you're acting, I can tell that you all know what's going on. But I would love to understand why we're hiding in this cave when we could be getting closer to the fort. None of us is tired, so that can't be it."

Breth gave her a sympathetic look, put his arm around her, and gently hugged her, careful not to smudge the woad on her naked body.

It felt wonderful, just the balm her frazzled nerves needed.

But Instead of answering her questions himself, he turned and looked to a young female fighter sitting next to them.

The woad-decorated naked blonde woman spoke when Jaelle turned and looked at her.

"Ah, but we are only three hours' walk away, including our hike down the mountain. We are quite close, thus our need to hide. Our attack wouldn't be much of a surprise if they saw us or heard us."

WHEN THE SUN was done setting, they all moved out of the cave, necessarily in single file. According to their plan, they split up into pairs and went their separate ways to the same location, for two reasons. One, this way if anyone was discovered, it would just be two people. The invaders would just think it was travelers, not a retalia-tory attack. Two, they had to move separately in order to surround the fort so that they could take as many Roman soldiers by surprise in their sleep as possible. They would time their attack by the height of the moon behind a certain tree they all knew as a landmark.

Jaelle and Breth were a pair, of course.

Before they got started, Breth showed her a dozen hand signals they could use to communicate silently, and while she concentrated on learning them, she was amused at the memory of movies showing modern-day soldiers doing the same thing. Once they had practiced those and she felt confident that they could communicate well, they headed on down the mountain.

It was cloudy tonight, and so barely any stars could be seen, but the moonlight penetrated the clouds and pervaded them. It made the Scottish skies look magical, while at the same time making shadows blurry so that the ground seemed less real.

Breth signaled that he was going to stop and she

should catch up with him so they could have a whispered conversation.

"You're doing a good job at being quiet, but you aren't as practiced as the clan. Please don't take this wrong way, but I need you to walk in my footsteps so that you don't step on leaves or twigs. They make noise. I know my strides are longer, so I'll shorten them for you. Agreed?"

She was already trying hard, and his words stung. She resisted wiping the tears that had sprung unbidden to her eyes.

But he did it for her, kissing them away and then holding her head tenderly.

She sat in silence for long time, letting him hold her and drawing strength from the feel of him. The smell of him.

At long last, she had her emotions under control. To show him she did, she whispered in jest.

"I suppose I can live with you being better at walking quietly, since I'm at least as good as you at fighting with the sword."

He squeezed her hand and looked into her eyes as he whispered.

"That you are. And I was trying my hardest. Ready?"

She was.

"Yes. Lead on, Macduff."

He looked at her quizzically.

She rolled her eyes at herself.

"It's a saying from five hundred years before my time. I'll explain it to you later."

"I'd like that."

He drew apart from her slowly and gently, then looked down at his feet and made a show of shortening his steps, then looked at her with a question in his eyes.

She nodded her agreement and did her best to walk in his footsteps.

He wrinkled his nose in a gesture that showed he was grateful, then turned and watched where he was going as he led her down the mountain and through the pass and up the hill from whose top they could peek through the bushes and see the fort below, on the other side of Hadrian's Wall.

TWENTY-ONE

In his favorite lookout spot at the top of the hill above the fort behind the bushes, Breth drew Jaelle close to him so that her eyes were looking as closely as possible at the same spot on the invaders' wall where he was looking. The sun was down, but the stones shone brightly in the moonlight. Just to be sure she knew where to look, he pointed, and the woad flock of egrets on his arm ruffled their feathers as he extended his arm out in front of the two of them.

So as not to be heard by the twelve barbarian guards marching in formation just on the other side of the wall, he whispered breathily in her ear, nuzzling her temple with his nose while he did so.

"Do you see those decorated wall stones on the top row over there, under the Sycamore tree?"

She leaned into him, making their heads graze together gently. Making the twin dragons on her chest take flight. And making the desire to kiss her almost irresistible.

Yeah, it was irresistible.

He kissed her hungrily this time, his desire held back only by the need to keep the woad on their bodies undisturbed. He cherished the kiss for what it was — passion in a stolen moment — and then resolutely but regretfully backed away so that they once more stood mostly apart behind the bushes, looking at the wall under the Sycamore tree.

Her head rubbed against his as she nodded gently.

"Yes, yes I see dark lines on those stones where the moonlight hits them just so."

He swallowed the sadness that he felt at what he had brought up to tell her. The time for sadness was passed, and he needed to move on with the life that was before him, not dwelling on the life that was behind. That was the way.

"Those are the stone carvings of Gisa's departed brother she was telling you about at the last wake. That's usually where I go over the wall, because the tree gives me a bit of cover. But the last time I was here, I was seen there, and so it's better if we go over somewhere else. I just wanted you to know that was where they were, so that if you ever got the chance you might look at them more closely. If you stay, of course we'll teach you how to decipher meaning from the pictures. It's very similar to the meanings of the pictures painted on our bodies right now — just not animated."

She started to turn toward him, but he caught her and held her firmly looking that way.

"It's better if you don't tempt me right now. We cannot disturb the woad, and you make it very tempting to do so."

She laughed ever so quietly, and he joined her for a moment. When they stopped, she spoke to him, still looking at the marked stones under the Sycamore tree.

"I'm staying for now, that's really all I can tell you."

He picked up some of her unusually thick — even if remarkably short — brown curly hair and let it spill out of his hand slowly.

"That's really all I can ask you to tell me. I'm happy."

She leaned her head in against his again, and they stood there with their foreheads touching, watching the wind make the Sycamore tree's branches wave in the moonlight, making shadows on the decorated wall. Sharing this view made him feel close to her.

She tapped the back of his hand with her finger.

"How long until we go?"

The moon wasn't quite in the agreed upon spot yet, but he would have to go more slowly than normal, with her along.

"It's time. The way is a bit tricky, but if you stay in my footsteps, you should make it silently."

She nodded and waited for him to start forward, her eyes fierce with the need for vengeance even though she'd only just met the members of his clan.

He stood and admired her for a moment. Her fierceness did something to him. There were female fighters in his clan, but Jaelle's passions surpassed those of any woman he had ever met. And he was up to the challenge of learning all of the many fighting styles she knew and someday besting her in a practice bout. He looked forward to that in a way he hadn't ever anticipated fighting practice.

Coming back to the moment, he led the way down through the gaps in the bushes to another easy place to climb over the wall. He waited for her to catch up to him and then gave her a boost up to the closest foothold in the wall, then lifted her to help her climb, whispering in her ear as she passed by him on the way up.

"I'll stay down here to catch you in case you fall. Wait for me at the top."

She nodded and gave him a quick kiss, then climbed up to the top of the ten foot wall.

And gasped.

The last thing he saw of her was the panic on her face as she was grabbed and pulled over onto the invaders' side.

Heart pounding, Breth turned around, grabbing his sword out of its sheath and raising it against the invaders he thought surely would be behind him.

But there were none.

Quick as the wind, he ran back up to the relative safety of the hilltop before yelling several times at the top of his lungs to the rest of his fighters.

"Retreat! It's a trap!"

He cursed himself and his preoccupation the whole

way to their meeting place and then was grateful to see that everyone else had made it out. He quickly explained what happened to Jaelle, and then he and all of his fighters started their retreat back to the safety of the cave, where they would plan their next attack.

TWENTY-TWO

J aelle barely had time to register what was happening before she found herself on the other side of the wall, stripped of the belt with its scabbard and the bag containing the helmet and with her hands bound behind her back, walking as fast as she could while being half-dragged by her elbow through the courtyard toward the door of the fort. By Nechtan.

There were others with them, but she didn't care who heard her. She knew she most definitely did not want to go inside that door. With any luck, the others didn't speak Pictish. She knew they were Roman soldiers by their attire — which to her modern sensibilities looked like little mini dresses — so she surmised that the language they were speaking was Latin — and she understood that, too, in addition to the Pictish.

Apparently unbeknownst to them.

"This female savage has more meat on her bones than most."

"Yes, but she is not for us. I hear Marcus asked for her."

"Too bad. All that blue stuff on her gives me ideas."

"It isn't the blue stuff that gives me ideas."

Crude laughter.

How charming.

But she concentrated on the druid, with whom she felt she might have a chance. Besides, he held the helmet bag in his other hand, along with her sword in its scabbard and her belt.

Hoping against hope that he didn't realize what he had, she made her face as appealing as she knew how and beseeched this member of Breth's clan.

"Please just let me go, Nechtan. Please."

But this just made the little man laugh at her. It was an evil laugh.

"You should have considered the relative power of the two men you had to choose from. You chose wrong."

Jaelle didn't even think.

Her mouth just went off, as it was wont to do.

"I wasn't making a choice. You didn't have a chance. I had already chosen Breth. And then you had to go butting in on something that wasn't your business."

There was that evil laugh again, and he jostled her by the elbow more than he needed to, making her trip. With her hands tied, the only thing that stopped her from falling flat on her face was his hold on her elbow, which was starting to ache.

But she wouldn't give him the satisfaction of calling

out in pain. A bit too late, she finally got control over her mouth.

This time his laugh was more mirthful — but still not sympathetic — as he prattled away at her in Pictish.

"And now you have butted into things that aren't your business, and look at the predicament you're in because of your meddling. You should have stayed outside the wall. I can't believe you showed up. I thought Breth would leave you back at the camp. You don't belong here. You don't have the slightest idea how far over your head you are here. It's no place for a woman from the future, where it is plain you are coddled. And Marcus has his eye on you anyway, but if he knew..."

Nechtan glanced around at the Roman soldiers walking with them, his look daring her to tell him — no, to beg him — to keep her secret.

Unwilling to beg, she stared at him. Her eyes sending a message.

Go ahead and tell them. See if they believe you.

His eyes on her were mocking, and they sent their own message.

Wait till you've been here a while. This place will wear you down. There will come a time when you beg me to tell them your secret on the off chance that they'll let you go.

What he said out loud was much less menacing.

"You're a stranger to this place, so it's understandable that you don't realize ... but you will."

They were at the door to the fort now, and he waited while one of the Roman soldiers pushed it open.

Normally, seeing men in mini dresses would've made her laugh, but since these men were menacing her, she just found their attire disgusting.

Once the door was open, she was dragged through it into a large room full of men — and one large rotund man wearing a toga and more jewelry than her mother had in her jewelry box.

Nechtan bowed to the floor to this man, dragging her down with him.

"Oh great Marcus, you sought to see the woman Jaelle, and look, I have brought her to you."

Marcus then addressed Jaelle directly.

"Look up at me, woman. I would see your face."

Nechtan jerked her upright.

While Marcus studied her, she saw his lecherous grin and was spooked to the point where she didn't have anything to say.

A first.

Of course, she had never been naked in a room full of men before, either. But she refused to slouch or otherwise try to hide what God had given her. She was not ashamed, so she would not act ashamed.

Marcus turned to three women seated on the floor who were wearing scarcely more than Jaelle.

"Up, up, up. Follow these men who take Jaelle to the quarters I have prepared for her. See that she gets all this... messy paste cleaned off of her."

The three women bowed their faces to the floor and then did as he asked, following as Nechtan handed her off to the Roman soldiers, who took her and the three women down the hall, unbound her hands, and pushed the four of them into a room, then locked the door from the outside.

Inside the room were a large Roman bathtub, a wardrobe, and a double bed. These things filled almost all the space available. The tub was already full of steaming water.

The woad was almost at the end of its magical life of two days anyway, so Jaelle didn't resist when the women ushered her up to the tub and gestured for her to get in. There was soap and a wash rag, and she got busy, refusing to let the women help her.

So instead they opened the wardrobe and showed her the contents — a surprising selection of clothing that didn't look complicated to put on. Just simple shifts, over-dresses, and scarves in many different colors. There were shoes as well, and it all looked like it would fit.

Good.

She wanted to be dressed the next time she saw any of the men. Being locked in this room without any of them here seemed a godsend, and she sank into the hot water and let it be a balm to relax her — as much as was possible under the circumstances.

But alas, this moment of peace had to end before the water even cooled.

The door opened and Marcus entered. He turned to the three women.

"Leave us."

Without a backward glance at Jaelle, the three rushed out, closing the door behind them.

Jaelle took advantage of the small time it took them to leave by getting out of the tub and drying off with one of the towels that sat nearby. She was nearly done when he turned back to her with that evil lecherous grin.

Trying her best to ignore him — and to keep herself covered — she finished drying off, wrapped the towel around her, then walked over to the wardrobe and calmly sifted through her clothing choices before selecting a saffron dress.

He didn't approach her, thank God, but stayed in the doorway leering at her.

"It's no use you know, hiding behind that towel. I've already seen it all."

Pretending to be very interested in the clothes, she selected three different overdresses and held them against the saffron before selecting a maroon one.

"Well, since you've 'been there, seen that,' you might as well turn around while I put these clothes on."

Marcus laughed his own brand of evil laugh. Nechtan's laugh was frightening enough in its bitterness at being rejected, but Marcus's laugh took evil to a whole new level. His was predatory. And obviously accustomed to getting his way.

The proud toga-wearing corpulent man strutted across the room as if he owned it — and perhaps as the commander of this post he came as close as one could come to owning a fort — clearly trying to make her shrink away from him.

She refused to do so.

He stopped five feet short of her and put his hands on

his hips — which looked really funny in a toga, making his nearness and his next words bearable.

"Nice try. But I like the view just fine facing this way."

She supposed it was a good thing she was in no mood to laugh. She didn't imagine he would take that well. As for herself, her hands trembled as she held the saffron dress over her head and put her arms through and pulled it down over the towel, then put the maroon dress on over the saffron dress and finally let the towel drop. But she maintained her dignity, neither cowering nor backing down.

And then he dropped the bomb.

"You'll enjoy our marriage, and it will start soon."

TWENTY-THREE

Jaelle passed most of the night doing the only thing she could think of that might do any good: carving her own version of this story into the base of the wall of her prison room with a nail file that had been left for her to use. It was much thicker than modern nail files and nicely suited to the purpose. She based her carvings on those she had admired in the cave, but she made them her own. This was a little because she hadn't been taught the Pictish system of pictures and a lot because she was a stubbornly independent person determined to show the world she had a mind of her own.

But mostly this was just her way of coping with being locked up. She thought if she didn't have something physical to do, she might just go mad. She carved until she was exhausted, then collapsed in the bed and fell asleep.

∾

KELSEY WAS SMILING when she first showed up in dreamland, smiling and dancing around. But then she saw Jaelle's face and came right down to earth.

Amber was along, of course, and ran over to Jaelle and hugged her protectively as the two of them sat on the bed with their legs crossed Indian style.

"Where are you? How did you get here? Where's Breth?"

Jaelle knew it was just a dream — well, not just a dream but not quite reality either — but even this virtual hug was infinitely more comfort than she'd had a moment ago. Aggravatingly, this allowed her resolve to crumble, and while she had held steadfast through talking with Marcus and Nechtan, this kindness from her friends made her blubber and cry.

She spoke through her sobbing, which made her sound like the drama queen she always resisted being, which in turn made her blubber even more. She could barely choke the words out.

"I was with Breth on an attack on the Roman fort just over the other side of the wall. That's where we are now. I climbed up on top of the wall in front of Breth and... You know what, just watch it in my memory. So much easier than trying to tell you."

So with the three of them sitting on the bed watching as if they were ghosts sitting on a ghost bed that floated around, Kelsey played Jaelle's memory of being captured and Nechtan's sneering derision at her plight as a modern woman — and Marcus's declaration that they were soon to be married.

Jaelle squirmed the whole time, finding it odd to be watching herself.

Kelsey's face was stricken.

"We have pictures of that helmet, Jaelle, and I will show them to the staff at Celtic University. I'll find someone who can help you. Just stay alive. Do what you have to do, but just stay alive. Promise me."

The choking and sobbing eased so that Jaelle could speak again, and she looked on her friend with the hope that she hadn't dared harbor before.

"Yes, yes I'll stay alive. Please do whatever you can to get me out of here."

Amber hugged her tighter.

"Of course she will."

There really wasn't anything more to say, so the three of them just spent the next little while holding each other while Amber and Kelsey stroked Jaelle's hair and told her it would be all right, that they would help her.

JAELLE WAS WOKEN up in what she presumed to be the morning — although she couldn't tell, because there weren't any windows in her room — by the three women who had helped her bathe the night before. They came in clucking and talking while they turned down the covers and scooted her over and moved her feet down to the floor.

As if that weren't bad enough, she didn't at all like the things they were saying in a language Jaelle associated with the Catholic Church more than anything. It was so odd to understand Latin.

"Get up, Jaelle. You're to be married now."

"Your wedding was going to be next week, but with the—"

The third woman cut the second woman off, shoving her and giving her a stern look.

"Marcus has decided he can't wait to marry you, so get up and get dressed so we can do what we do."

The first two women got out a long white woolen blanket and walked to opposite sides of the room, stretching it out.

At first this puzzled Jaelle, but then she realized the white blanket was the makings of a toga that they were going to wrap around her.

A toga just like the one Marcus wore.

Wonderful.

Woman three was setting out a bunch of clay pots and handmade makeup brushes on the half of the bed Jaelle wasn't sitting on.

But there wasn't any joy in these preparations. The three women were clearly just obeying orders they were afraid not to follow. And who could blame them, what with being locked in rooms and all?

The first woman had finished walking to her corner of the room and turned to beckon Jaelle over her shoulder.

"We must make you beautiful — so quick, quick, quick, get up."

Somehow, the bath had been drawn again before Jaelle woke up — which must've meant carrying in buckets of water, because there wasn't any plumbing in the room. She had a large earthenware jar under her bed as testimony to this, and it had been convenient.

However, Jaelle was stubbornly unwilling to be that clean for a wedding she didn't want. She declined to get in the bath but just scooped up some water and washed the sleep out of her eyes before turning to the three women and giving herself over to their care.

"Go ahead, make me beautiful."

The first two women removed Jaelle's saffron and maroon dresses and then wrapped the long white wool blanket around her and shaped it into a toga, pleating it just so and tucking it in here and putting it over her arm there and fastening it with a brooch.

In an odd way, the toga reminded Jaelle of the great kilts the guys had worn at the Renaissance faire.

But this went down to the floor and made walking difficult — unless one walked in a stately manner. Maybe that was the point of the cumbersome thing, to make one pause and consider one's appearance before moving or speaking — or even breathing, truly.

The toga covered her well though, and for that she was grateful.

Going naked with just the woad paint had been close to unbearable in the company of Breth and his clan fighters who were doing the same. She hadn't really stopped to think that she would actually be in front of the

Roman soldiers looking like that. Well, she'd never thought she would be alone when she made her bare-skin entrance into the domain of foreign men.

It just went to show: one should always pick one's outfit carefully, with every possible situation in mind.

Next, these captive women applied cosmetics to Jaelle's face in an amount that astonished her. She had thought makeup was a modern invention. Not so. Why hadn't any of this been in the history books she'd read so studiously? Maybe she needed to read some historical memoirs — if any written by women from this time could be found. Slim chance of that. Well, maybe in Rome itself, where some women were more respected.

But first she needed to find Nechtan and wrench that helmet from his little meddling hands and get away from this awful situation.

He was sure to be at her wedding ceremony, gloating over her fate. Wasn't he? Well, she would plan on it. And as soon as she saw him, she would just run over to him and grab the helmet — which she was sure he would have in his possession, knowing how valuable it was.

Yeah, that's just what she would do.

The three women rushed through their preparations, and all too soon they were banging on the door, which was still locked from the outside.

"We're finished!"

"She's ready!"

"Open up!"

Two men unnecessarily haggled the three women

away down the hall. The women weren't resisting, but the men were making a big show of urging them on anyway, probably enjoying the process.

This fort was not a good place.

Two other men haggled Jaelle down the long dark windowless hall into the courtyard, where a toga'd officiant was waiting. Oddly, there was nobody else out in the courtyard except the officiant and Marcus. The men deposited Jaelle in front of the officiant, waited for a nod from Marcus, and then went off toward the gateway outside.

The officiant stood there looking bored, with his eyes far off in the distance over the wall of the fort into the mountains.

Lovely.

She was practically alone with Marcus.

Her mouth didn't like that either.

"How do I rate a toga anyway, Marcus? What makes you think I'm marriage material?"

He gave her a shrewd but amused look.

"Well the way I see it, Breth is nobility of a sort among his people — and he chose you, which means you are worthy of him. Oh, don't try to deny it. I saw the way he looked at you. He's very smitten, you know. Therefore, in the Roman way, your status carries over into our society, thus making you eligible as my bride."

Well that wasn't the answer she wanted.

"Nobility isn't all it's cracked up to be."

He laughed.

"Don't tell me you would rather join the ranks of slaves."

She put on a mockery of being shocked, placing her palm on her chest.

"You mean it matters what I would prefer? Well in that case, let me and all the other women go. In fact, pack up all your stuff and go back to Rome where you belong."

He gave her that evil grin again, laughing at her, rather than with her.

"Ironically, before you showed up, that's exactly what I wanted. But now I think I might enjoy staying here and fathering children."

Incredulous, she smiled on one side of her mouth, lowering the same eyebrow at him while throwing her hand up to the side.

"You only picked me because you knew it would break Breth's heart, so let's not pretend you're actually interested in me for my charm and wit."

At this, Marcus threw back his head and laughed.

"I'm definitely starting to enjoy myself. Now let's get on with the ceremony so we can get on with... the rest of it."

Casting about for anything to keep this wedding from going forward — not that she would feel obligated to honor a marriage taken under duress — she grabbed the sword the officiant wore and drove it hard at Marcus.

At first he just stood there with his jaw dropping.

"You dare?"

But then drawing his own sword, Marcus came at her with a calm seriousness that was more frightening than it would have been if he had lost control of his temper. His considerable weight was a large disadvantage, though. He was slow going.

Guessing that most of the reason he was going slow — aside from the toga — was that he knew his weight would cause him to tire quickly, Jaelle retreated across the courtyard, forcing him to run after.

It worked.

He was out of breath and huffing after her.

She checked the officiant, but he was still acting bored, as if he had no idea what was going on. Maybe he was on drugs. Or maybe he knew what was good for him.

Resisting the urge to laugh at Marcus and thus give him a chance to catch up to her, Jaelle pushed her advantage and rushed at him with her sword high in the air and chopped down.

Wheezing, Marcus raised his sword and blocked her.

Hearing battle sounds outside the fort, Jaelle's spirits rose. Breth!

She continued to criss cross the courtyard, hacking and slashing at Marcus and making him run after her for fear she would escape in the absence of his soldiers, who must be outside fighting. She would let Marcus just about catch up to her, and then she would turn around and rush at him, forcing him to stop and pivot and raise his sword in defense.

She gave him no opportunities for offense whatsoever. She was cocky, but she wasn't stupid. He was much stronger than she, even if he was in terrible shape. No, her two advantages were speed and endurance, and she used them.

It seemed like forever that this running about continued, but finally the Pictish warriors rallied into the courtyard.

And there was Breth, calling her name.

"Jaelle!"

She continued to fight Marcus off until Breth got there to take over the job for her, to finish it. She hadn't killed anyone yet, and she knew she could, but she would rather not.

At last, Breth took over.

Jaelle was just standing there admiring Breth's sword-fighting form — and watching with abated breath to make sure he was winning and she didn't have to move in and help him — when out of the corner of her eye she saw Nechtan, running at her and swinging the bag with the helmet in it.

If he threw the helmet, only God knew where it would end up.

She couldn't let the druid do that.

Tearing her eyes away from Breth — whom she only now realized she must already love in some crude primal way — Jaelle prepared to push the little druid to the ground and stop him from throwing the helmet over the wall.

Only that wasn't what Nechtan was doing.

He was making that gesture he had made a few days earlier in the sacred grove, when he had animated the vines in retaliation against Deoord's vines. It had been an impressive and powerful show of natural power.

Jaelle braced herself for the onslaught.

But the vines didn't come.

Looking down, she saw why. Of course. The courtyard of the fort was paved with stones cut by man. The ground wasn't in its natural state. As she looked, though, odd strains of moss hurriedly grew up out of the cracks between the stones.

She smirked at the little man.

"Really? That's all you can muster, moss?"

Laughing a mocking laugh at the impotent druid, she turned to face him.

And then she understood the moss. It was slick, and in her haste to push the little man over, she slipped.

The druid was swinging the bag in an arc that would make the heavy iron helmet connect with Jaelle's head.

She raised her arms up from their position designed to push the little man over.

But it was too late.

Passing over her arms, the bag with the helmet in it completed its arc and swung toward her head.

As she fell from slipping on the moss, Jaelle looked for the man she admired more than any she had ever met. The man she was only just beginning to get to know. And love. The man she wanted to be with.

There he was, still alive.

Still fighting.

And oh, thank God, he was winning, stabbing Marcus fatally.

Good.

The helmet hit her just before she would have banged into the paving stones of the courtyard. A blinding flash of pain took over her whole head just before she blacked out.

TWENTY-FOUR

J aelle woke up in her basement with a pounding headache. Looking around at all the empty beer bottles, she groaned. Would she never learn?

And she hadn't gotten much work done. She was still surrounded by all of John's boxes full of who knew what. She was wearing the clothes she had dreamed of wearing and the Roman helmet she remembered taking out of one of the boxes. Huh. She must have taken these clothes out of the boxes, too.

Feh, this helmet was heavy! How she had managed to fall asleep in it was beyond her. She took it off and put it back in the box.

But what a dream!

She paused to relive it for a moment.

Naked warriors and mini-skirted Roman soldiers, druids who pulled vines up out of the ground to tangle people and then betrayed you to the Romans for not choosing them over the sexy warrior, a broch full and complete with five floors and a roof that also acted as a chimney?

Wow.

She'd always had a vivid imagination, but last night it was working overtime. Ugh, too bad that dreamy Breth wasn't real. Talk about a man!

The cold hard cement floor brought her back to reality.

What time was it, anyway?

Huh, her phone was out of juice. It had been fully charged just last night. She went upstairs and plugged it in to charge while she took a much needed shower. How had she managed to get so sweaty while sleeping in the cold basement?

Once plugged in, her phone came to life.

Well that was odd. She could have sworn it was the twenty first when she went to sleep, but no. Wow, she must have really overdone it with the beer this time. Today was the thirty first. And she had work. Her bus came in forty-five minutes.

She took off the old fashioned clothes she had dreamed about. She would put them back in the basement later. Right now she just barely had time to get ready for work. She did her normal bathroom routine, threw on some jeans — her second favorite pair, because her favorites weren't in her closet. They must be in the laundry. No time to go back down to the basement and see. She stuck her half-charged phone in her purse with her overdue library book and skedaddled, just making it to the bus stop in time.

During the half hour ride, she got out her phone to answer her messages. Whoa. She had way too many for this time of the morning. She would tackle them at lunch, and — oh, there was one from Amber. On seeing it, shame hit Jaelle. She hadn't left things that well with her oldest friend.

She should call Amber, but not right now. Wait until she had enough time to do a call justice.

For now, she prepared an email:

Amber, let's talk. I don't feel like we left things well last night. Sorry I was so short with you about how happy you are with Tomas. Glad you guys are happy. Just understand that I'm still upset...

Jaelle paused at that.

She wasn't upset about John anymore. No, she was upset that the man she had dreamed about, Breth, was just a dream and not real.

She relaxed and leaned her head back against the cushioned bus seat, letting her mind wander to that wonderful dream. Now there was a man! Strong, able, and decisive, yet still tender and considerate. He was someone she really wanted to get to know better.

She laughed at herself, startling the woman sitting next to her on the bus, who seemed to be checking if Jaelle was one of those crazies.

Jaelle held the phone up and jiggled it a little bit. She was telling a lie, but she really didn't want to get into it.

She had to get off the bus soon and wouldn't have time to do the story justice.

And then her mouth went off anyway.

"I had a dream last night about the perfect man. He was gorgeous, and he understood me. And then I woke up."

The woman smiled in sympathy.

"Don't worry. You'll find the right one someday."

Jaelle smiled in thanks.

"That was nice of you to say. Well, you have a nice day. This is my stop."

She gestured toward the door with her head.

The woman smiled kindly.

"You as well. Things will look up, you'll see."

Feeling oddly comforted, Jaelle got off the bus and headed over to Vivian's diner. It was true. Things were looking up. It was good news that she was finally getting over John, even if it had taken a dream to help her get over him.

But feh.

When she went into the diner, she saw Richard, a fussy, long-haired, bearded man who had brought exhibits to the museum before. Funny, she hadn't ever noticed just how tall and broad Richard was. She thought of him as a mousy man, but he made the diner chair look like a toy.

He waved and gestured her over to his table.

That was odd. He hadn't ever been friendly before, just told her about the new exhibits along with all the other tour guides.

Vivian came up and put an arm around Jaelle.

"Hi, hun." And then under her breath, "Is that guy over there bothering you? Just say the word and I'll get rid of him."

Jaelle chuckled.

"No, it's okay. He's associated with the museum. Going to have to talk to him when I get over there anyway, so may as well start now. Maybe that will make things less rushed than they usually are, although I doubt it."

Vivian scrunched her nose up at Jaelle in a look of sympathy and then nodded and walked away with the coffeepot to fill someone's cup.

"Okay, just remember I have your back."

Jaelle returned the gesture.

"Thanks."

Steeling herself for some tedium during what was usually reading time, Jaelle went over and stood by Richard's table.

"Hello. I guess you have a new exhibit for us, huh?"

Richard gestured for Jaelle to sit with him, another first.

And his eyes pierced right into her.

"Aye, and it will interest you, I think. It's about the history of Hadrian's Wall. It includes some actual pieces from the Wall, and they have markings you may recognize."

"Why would I recognize them?"

"Oh, several reasons. Don't you know this man, for example?"

He showed her a close-up picture of part of his exhibit. There was a carving of a warrior smaller in stature than some others. And the way he wielded his sword was unique. Because John had invented it.

Deirdre and Galdus travel to the time of Hadrian's Wall

Leif

Lauren and Galdus trick two friends into time traveling

Taran

Lauren surrenders to Galdus - or does she?

Luag

Lauren's friend Katherine takes on a laird's court

To be notified of new releases

sign up at

janestain.com

As Cherise Kelley:

Dog Aliens 1, 2 & 3: A Dog Story

My Dog Understands English!

How I Got Him to Marry Me

High School Substitute Teacher's Guide

AFTERWORD

Hi,

Thank you for reading this book all the way to the end. I hope you liked it.

I was 19 when I first heard of the druids and the picts and the celts. They caught my imagination so strongly that I painted myself blue for Halloween that year and worked at Sears that way for the day!

If you did like Time of the Celts, will you please take a moment to write at least 20 words in a review, telling other readers what you liked?

I appreciate it,

Jane

Made in the USA
Middletown, DE
08 September 2021